Ken Lansdowne

The Fairy Dust KILLER

A Bent Mystery
3

H Publishing
Denver, Colorado

PUBLISHERS NOTE: This is a work of fiction. Names, characters, places and incidents are the product of the authors imagination and are used fictitiously. Any resemblance to actual persons living or dead, events or locals are entirely coincidental.

No part of this book may be reproduced in any form or by any means—including photocopying or electronic reproduction—without permission from the publisher.

Library of Congress Cataloging in Publication Data
The fairy dust killer: a novel/ Ken Lansdowne
    p.   cm.
  ISBN 0-9740853-4-0/978-0-9340853-4-0
  1. Title.

1st Printing 2009
Kindle edition 2011
Copyright © 2007 by Ken Lansdowne

Published by H Publishing
605 South Clinton Street
Denver, Colorado 8024

H Publishing

Printed in USA

Prologue

It floated among the detritus around the piers situated at the end of New York's Christopher Street. After being in the water for so many hours it had begun to bloat. Open whip wounds on the back had caught twigs, small pieces of tinfoil, gum wrappers, a used condom. Any blood that had poured from the wounds had long washed away with the river's current. The upper limbs, tied behind its back, had the nails pulled out and the pads eradicated. The head had no tongue. It's genitalia were missing—crudely cut away. A pale lilac paint, applied haphazardly, had peeled and chipped from the skin. Gulls had picked at the open wounds, flying away with any loose bits they could salvage.

The rhythm of the river's waves caused the body to slam up against the water's edge, then would wash it back out. And bring it in once more to hit against the mossy rocks along the waterline.

It had turned out to be one of the first sun filled days of an eagerly awaited summer, so men from all over the neighborhood had pulled out shorts, muscle T's, sunglasses, and swimsuits to promenade and be seen cruising along the streets of Greenwich Village, Especially along the main drag.

At the bottom of Christopher two men sat together on a railing next to the West Side Highway man-watching away the afternoon, Currently they were focused on a studly specimen, in a deliciously skimpy swimsuit, sunbathing out on the pier.

He was well muscled and slathered in oil, shining in the sun, at the beginning of his first important tan of the season. A winter's worth of gym workouts assured the exhibitionist in him that he was being watched. A sensual thrill ran through him because of it. He liked being watched—very much—otherwise there would have been no reason for a winter's worth of workouts.

His hand rubbed across his chest, around his nipple, and down to his stomach. He outlined each hard ab muscle, and then lingered a second at the bellybutton. He let his hand go lower to cup at his crotch. He relished the feeling as blood rushed in to engorge his member. He slid a finger under the swimsuit leg seam, lifted, and felt the air hit his cock as it was released from its confines. He wrapped his hand around it and began to rub its length in well practiced manipulations.

A surreptitious glance told him that the men behind were still watching. They couldn't take their eyes off him! A shiver ran along his spine at the erotic feelings this knowledge engendered for him.

Knowing these men lusted for him made his

hand stroke faster. Another glance back and he saw that one of the men had stood and was pointing toward him. Great! That meant there could be even more attention on him. Yeah! Get a crowed, baby!

Now both men were standing. For a better view? Well, watch this! His cock was harder than he could ever remember. The veins along it pulsed as the blood flowed faster through his body. His head felt like it would burst. He felt a rush, a heat that must be satisified. His hand moved faster.

The two men behind him were yelling something, but he couldn't hear what it was. Now they were coming toward him. To join him? This could be hot! One of the men was almost to where he was lying. Coming closer, as was his cock.

Then the man went past him and headed directly for the water. The second man reached him and stopped.

"Put that thing away, you jerk-off," he said. "The cops are gonna be here any minute. There's a dead guy floating in the water down there!"

Chapter 1

Len Matthews was, as usual, running hard to catch up. It had been a real trial for him to break long-standing habits and show up for his appointments on time. He congratulated himself because tonight, for once, he had given himself enough time to take care of his errand and still arrive at the theatre well before curtain.

He stopped at the Korean deli on the corner where he picked out a bunch of white and rust mums, then he added greenery and pale yellow jonquils to a great many smiles and nods from the deli owner. He paid an exorbitant amount of money for the flowers—which explained the smiling and nodding—then took off for his nightly walk to the West Side of New York City.

This walk was his way of having some time to himself, preparation time if you will. to gear up and inhibit Gray, the character he played in *The Greenhouse Murder*, his show currently running on Broadway.

Before he made the turn to go across town

to the theater district, he turned onto an East Forties side street and went mid-block to the entrance of a small nightclub. He entered, left the flowers he'd bought in a drinking glass on the piano, and then continued on his way to the West Side.

By ten-thirty PM Len was taking his bows to loud applause. As it faded and the curtain fell he made his way to his dressing room with a single purpose in mind. Remove his make-up, change clothes, and get to the Four-Two-Nine,

JB—or Jeremy Bent if you want to be formal—was sitting at Len's make-up table and looked like he might be a hinderence to that goal.

"And what can I do you, mon friend? No place else to hang about?"

JB was an angelar man, long and lean with broad shoulders and a narrow waist. A slight touch of grey at the temples made him seem daddy-ish, even sexy, to a certain element of the gay population. He was the writer of the play Len had just finished performing. He was also Len's best friend in the whole world. They had a vast history between them, including a long ago period when they had lived together as lovers.

JB said, "Actually, no, but now that I'm in that big old apartment by myself I was feeling kind of lonely.**** He looked up to see if Len was the least bit sympathetic. He didn't appear to be the least bit interested.

JB continued defensively. "Well, with Toby

****To find out how these circumstances came about see *A Murderous Ball Of Fluff*, #2 in the Bent Mystery series off to California, abandoning me so to speak, and me having to take over as landloard of the building while he's gone...I mean the books are a total mess...and I was having trouble coming up with a twist for the new novel I'm stuck on. So, I came over to check on the play...and to see you, of course." JB even managed to make his bottom lip tremble a tiny bit.

"Stop for crips sake," Len said. "I'm not buying it. For one thing you and Toby have been busted up for months. You knew he was going to Hollywood weeks ago, so he has hardly abandoned you. You should be used to his absence by now. As to your writing problems they usually last about ten seconds. And need I remind you there are people in this town who would truck with the devil himself to live in that huge apartment you're complaining about. So get off the pity pot, perk up, and get the hell out of my chair."

JB quickly stood.

Len took his place, then removed his coat, his tie and his shirt. He held them out for JB to take from him. JB took the clothing and went over to a wardrobe rack standing against the wall.

Len looked at JB's reflection in the mirror. "You know, sweetie, what you really need is some fun. If you are primarily involved with only the tasks at hand day after day then dullness will be the inevitable result."

JB put a wire hanger into the shirt and hung it up. "Gee, Len, you mean more fun than getting to be your valet?"

"No, that's a bonus just for you." Len opened up a jar of *Abolene* and smeared it on his face. He then took several tissues from a box and began to wipe away his make-up. "What I mean is for you to come out with me tonight. I'm going to this little club I found. The Four-Two-Nine. It's in our neighborhood. We could have dinner, talk, enjoy the singing."

JB hung up Len's coat, then turned back to face him. He asked, "Is this the place where you've been hiding out for the last few weeks? I was wondering what you'd found to keep you so busy. You haven't been around your apartment at all." He paused a second. "Singing? They sing at this place? It's not one of those karoake places is it? You know I can't sing, Len."

"No, JB, it's something you don't see much of any more. It's one of those old-fashioned kind of piano bars. Only the regulars will get a chance to stand up and sing, so you shouldn't worry yourself. They have this really terrific piano player. His name is Cubby Curtis. Cubby knows all the lyrics to every song for practically every show ever writttten. And the place is lots of fun. Do you want to come with me or not?"

"Are you kidding? Anything that can get the blasé and jaded Len Matthews to sound even this enthusiastic I've got to see."

"Okay then. I'll get dressed, and then we can grab a cab."

"It amazes me that you are willing to walk all the way over here every single night, all the way across town, but then have to take a cab to get back. What's up with that?"

Len shrugged. "One's work. The other is my off-time. There is a difference." JB lookied doubtful. "Well, it makes sense to me."

"Len, when the press makes the ungodly fuss it does over some thin-skinned, egotistic millionaire's affair with a chorus girl it makes sense to you." He paused then asked. "So you've been going to this nightclub every night? Is that a good idea?"

JB was remembering all to well Len's past experiences with bars and alcohol, and the effect it had on his life. It came near to ruining his career. The last few months had been relatively calm since Len had spent some time in a rehab and had started going to AA meetings.

Len gave JB's mirror reflection an icy look. "Thank you for your concern, but I think I have it well under control. I am fine."

"Okay. Just asking. But set my mind at ease, will you? When did you go to your last meeting?"

"JB, the AA program says that getting sober is a bridge back to life. Well, I'm getting on with my life. If that's all right with you?"

"Fine. Forget I asked. Do what makes your world a happy one."

"I have, and I will."

Chapter 2

The Four-Two-Nine was one of those nightclubs that managed to keep reinventing itself for every new era that came along. It started as a speakesy during Prohibition, got down and dirty in the Forties, was a beatnik hangout in the Fifties, and a chic little jazz club in the Sixties. Then it morphed into a gay hustler bar for the next decade. This season it had managed to keep the moneyed part of that same gay clientele by becoming a piano bar and restaurant. Having gone through almost as many names as incarnations it had settled on its address as it's current identity. 4-2-9. The numbers were painted in fancy script on the awning that covered the entrance.

Len pulled open the hobnailed covered door to let JB enter.

Taking a moment to let his eyes adjust JB could see a long wooden bar running down one side, backed by the buildings last remaining element of its speakeasy days—a long mirror etched with leaping fawns and Deco style convoluted lines. Three horseshoe banquettes with tiny tables in their curves ran along the other wall.

Giant florist made arrangements of twigs and blooms separated each of the booths. Thirty feet down the narrow space, across from the end of the bar, was a platform that held an upright piano and a microphone. Beyond that was the dining room. Everything was lit by indirect light with the resulting impression that you had stepped into another dimension, without time or very much substance.

Len put his hands on JB's shoulders and whispered, "Didn't I tell you it was nice?"

Len maneuvered JB toward the bar. Pulling out a stool and indicating JB should sit Len continued, "You order us something to drink. I'll have a cranberry and soda. And I'll see about getting us something to eat. Then I want you to meet Cubby." Len was off, which left JB to order. The server, a standard gay bartender type—young, handsome, muscled, terrific looking in a tight T-shirt and up-lighting—took JB's order then asked, "Are you a friend of Len's?"

"Yes I am. Does Len come in here often?"

"Lately he has. Nice guy too. He and Cubby have been working together."

"Cubby?" That was the second or third time JB had heard that name in the last hour.

The youth looked down the bar and nodded toward someone standing at the end. "Cubby. Right there. He's our star attraction."

JB looked in the diredtion indicated and spotted this Cubby person. He was older—much too old to be still called Cubby—than JB or Len. Mid-fifties maybe, but good looking and still putting up a valiant effort against age and its effects. His skin, smooth and pink cheeked, was a testament to the benifits of using a daily moisturizer. His dark hair, generously sprinkled with grey, was worn in a blown dry style that was flattering if not a bit outdated. He had a strong looking face, the jaw of which had started to jowl slightly at the edges. Deep lines at his eyes and mouth indicated a man of considerable humor

If his clothes, a dinner jacket woven to alternate between a sea green and an electric blue, and his jewelry—a heavy gold bracelet, a multi-dialed watch, and an over sized pinky ring—were all a bit flashy, JB hoped it was more a reflection of his job than his taste. He stood completely at ease with a drink in his hand talking to another of the bartenders.

Then Len stepped up behind him, said a few words in his ear, and the two of them headed down the bar toward where JB was sitting.

As Cubby got closer JB saw that what he had taken to be humor lines at eye and lip might have more to do with dissolute living than any laughter the man might enjoy. The pink cheeks turned out to be more the result of a network of small broken veins than good health.

The bartender put down the drinks JB ordered just as Len started his introduction. JB picked up Len's drink, handed it over to him, and turned to Cubby. "Nice to meet you," he said. They shook hands. Cubby's pinky ring cut into JB's fingers.

JB started to understand the reason for the man's bright clothing when Cubby began to speak. His voice was kept very soft—you had to lean forward to hear him in the noise of the bar. It was also placed in the back of his throat, which gave it a liquid phlegmy sound. The words were spoken without inflection, almost a monotone. Cubby's clothing then was meant to give him some color, to make him livlier than he actually was. To use a Sixties expression, he appeared to be so 'laid-back" he was almost comatose.

He didn't say much to JB, except to explain he must get ready for his next set and how nice it was to meet him. Then he left and walked away toward the kitchen.

"I got us a table for dinner. The food is just okay. Mostly snack stuff. But the food isn't really the main reason people come here." Len escorted JB back toward the dining room.

JB asked, "What is the main reason then? Beyond your regulation standard issue gay bar scene, this doesn't have much to offer."

A voice on the sound system announced the musical stylings of Mr. Cubby Curtis. The entire place exploded in raucous applause.

Cubby, lit by a follow spot, walked by JB and Len's table headed for the platform. Basking in the sound of many hands clapping he stepped up beside the piano and took a bow as the overhead lights—a bank of pink gels—went on. He sat to play.

With a live microphone situated an inch from his mouth Cubby's voice transformed. It became sexy, even seductive, giving him an appeal ceratinly not obvious on first meeting. While fingering the keys of the piano he introduced a song from *Redhead,* an almost forgotten Gwen Verdon musical from the Nineteen-fifties. His singing voice was a sort of suto-Bobby Short with a strong hint of Eartha Kitt. It sinuously grabbed at you on the first note and didn't let go as he gave delicate shading and deep meaning to each note of the song.

"Wow," JB exclaimed. "He's really good."

Len nodded. "Now you know the reason people come here."

Cubby went on to sing a few more numbers. When the waiter came over to take their food orders it was hamburgers and fries for both. Then the waiter disappeared into the kitchen as Cubby began to sing another song.

"Uh, Len, the bartender said you and Cubby are working together. What's that about?"

"That bartender has a big mouth."

"And it makes him very popular," JB retorted. "You and Cubby?"

"Well, you know I said I wanted to do musicals?"

"Yes."

"Cubby has been working with me to help me develop my singing voice. I've been taking lessons."

"No kidding?"

Cubby finished his song and leaned into the microphone. "We are very lucky tonight," he said. "We have a Broadway star here with us, and I think if given the right encouragement we can get him to sing."

Cubby looked over at Len. "The star of *The Greenhouse Murder*. Mr. Len Matthews."

"You're going to sing?," JB asked.

Len stood. "It looks like it, doesn't it."

Len went to the platform, took the microphone, had a few quiet words with Cubby, and after a florish of an intro, went into a lively version of the old Fanny Brice song *I'd Rather Be Blue*.

JB sat, his mind numb with amazement, watching his best friend—singing in a nightclub—like some character out of an Isherwood story. One must learn to hold on tightly to the safety bar on Len's personal roller coaster. This was just another loop-de-loop on the ride that was his life.

Len finished his song, bowed to the audience and came back to the table, sitting once again across from JB. At approximately the same instant he sat, he said, "Well? What did you think?"

"Len, I've heard you sing before. Of course the water from the shower tended to drown out the worst notes."

"JB, come on. I want your opinion. Why do you think I brought you here tonight?"

"I was wondering that exact same thing. Why?"

Cubby had finished up his set and left the platform to come back to the dining room. He went to JB and Len's table where he took a seat across from them.

Len threw up his hands. "My God, you can sometimes be so dense. I'm taking lessons. I just sang..." He huffed. "Damn it, JB, do you think I can do musicals?"

"I don't see why not. If Rex Harrison, Rock Hudson, and even Raquel Welsh can, there's no reason you can't. You aren't built like Raquel, or even Rock, but you have a good character voice. You probably won't become the next Mandy Patinkin, but you can carry a tune,"

"That's exactly right," Cubby added. "It's what I've been telling him all along. He has a good chance to do musicals if he'll work on it. But what's more important is we have to get him seen." Cubby looked over at Len. "By the way, the flowers are beautiful."

"Your welcome. I thought you would like them. They're for thank you."

"You always know the right thing to do, don't you?" He leaned over as if to peck Len on the cheek, but instead picked up Len's drink and took a sip.

"What the hell is that?"

"Cranberry and soda. Why?"

"It tastes like leftover sauce from Thanksgiving. It could use some kick. Man, you are such a goodie-two shoes." He stood up. "I'm getting a real drink. He turned to JB. "Are you okay?"

"I'm fine." Cubby headed for the bar. JB chuckled. "What he doesn't know, Len, is that there are some very dark socks under those two shoes. Right?" He leaned in. "Now, Mr. Two-Shoes, would you care to explain what this is all about? And while you're at it, explain the flowers on the piano too. I have received flowers from you only once in all the time we've known each other, and that was when I was in Lenox Hill to get my gall bladder removed. Now what is going on? If I have to guess I'll come up with one tacky scenario, you know."

"Just get the name spelled right."

"Seriously, Len. What?"

"Okay. I wanted you here so you could hear me sing, because...I mean, so I could ask..."

"Uh-oh. This sounds like it's going to cost me money."

"Actually, it's about how much you value your time and talent."

"Huh?"

"Well, Cubby says I have to get seen by people who do musicals, and to do that he's found a place down in the Village that wants to book my cabaret act for a two week run."

"That sounds like a good idea."

"It is a chance for agents to see me doing something new, and it could lead to some important auditions. But it also presents a problem."

"Oh? What?"

"I don't have a cabaret act."

"And you want me to?"

"Write me an act. You are a writer, JB. And a good one too. Especially now, since you're in the running for a Tony award."

"Running, schumming. It's the nomination that counts. I haven't got that yet." JB thought for a moment. "Len, I've never done anything like this before. I haven't the slightest idea of what's required."

"Not a problem. Between your writing, Cubby's experience on the club scene, and my show biz pizzazz we are bound to come up with something terrific."

"And when do Judy and Mickey show up to turn the barn into a theater?"

Arms inside please, the ride is about to begin.

Chapter 3

If you happen to be a gay man in America you have basically two choices. One coast or the other. West or East. San Francisco or New York. Castro or Christopher. And, in actual fact, they are mostly interchangable. Put a Castro gay on Christopher and he'll fit right in and vice-versa. Dress alike—look alike. It's a sort of franchise thing. Like a gay Gap.

JB came up the subway stairs onto Sixth Avenue where a thin park and the Stonewall Inn were located right behind the station. He crossed the street, walked past the red painted Village Cigar store, past Boots and Saddles—called Bras and Girdles by the locals—and headed further down the street to where Len had arranged to meet him.

It was a pretty day and since the street denizens were also pretty JB slowed, the better to enjoy the passing parade. All kinds, all sizes, all ages, all attractive, all gay. Laid out end to end they would probably reach—for each other.

JB found the place he was looking for a few blocks down. The front was a multi-colored old brick facade on a two-story Victorian building. The door was situated to the left with a light bulb encircled announcement board hung just to the right of that. The board was capped with the bar's name spelled in flashing bulbs—Cherries. There were flyers pinned to the glass covered corkboard below. The flyers advertised whichever act was next appearing in the bar's showroom.

JB pulled open the front door. It led to a small landing which faced another door. The double doors were meant to protect patrons during the snow storms and cold winds of New York winters. Opening that second door found another landing attached to a wide set of wooden stairs leading down.

At the bottom was a narrow longish brick walled basement room. An upright piano stood on a small platform across from the stairs on the opposite wall. There was not a seat or table in sight, only a thin shelf to sit drinks on which ran around the walls at waist height. Light filtered in from a iron grated set of windows running at street level across the front. The walls were painted cherry red—bing not maraschino. There were also hundreds of antique mirrors in unmatched gold gilt frames hung high and low—everywhere.

The bar itself was at the far end of the room and ran across the back wall. Stools covered in red and black vinyl material ran the length of it. Over to the right of the bar, behind a half wall and circled with more blinking lights was the entrance to the showroom. On the other side of the half wall was another doorway with stairs leading up. At the top of them was an outside street level deck used when weather permitted.

Len, currently the only customer, was sitting center bar. He waved JB back, then gave his order to the person working behind the bar. "I'll have a Roy Rogers, please, with a Dale Evens chaser."

The bartender was almost worth wasting a couple of daytime hours sitting in a Village gay bar for. A sight to behold he should have been featured on Gray Line Tours of the West Village.

He was wearing drag. To be more precise, he was wearing a longhaired shaggy hot pink fake-fur completely over-the-top of any line you care to choose kind of drag.

He was dressed in a thigh length great coat made of the same fuzzy material usually used for stuffed animals and toilet seat covers. This Muppet-like garment was worn over a pink shiny sequin covered sweater with a pink and brown nubby tweed mini-skirt. Fishnet hose and calf-high pink plastic cha-cha boots finished off his *Pepto-Bismol* color coordinated ensemble. His wig, dyed the same hot pink as the coat, was parted down the middle and pulled into cone shaped obtrusions on each side of his head, out of which fell long cascading pink ponytails. Hung off of each of his ears were brush-your-shoulder sized pink plastic hoops.

This was not glamour drag. This drag was designed to cause outright laughter. To amaze at the preposterousness of it, and to shock uptight little old ladies and piss-off any odd conserveatives hanging around. This was drag to put the fun back into dressing up.

"Well, what do you think?"

JB looked after the bartender. "I think that if that guy doesn't watch out, Elmer's gonna come in here and shoot himself a big bright pink fuzzy wabbit."

"I was talking about the bar, but he is a

hoot isn't he?"

"And a half. I wonder if he can get me something to drink?" JB held up a finger and mouthed the word "beer".

The drag nodded. Moments later he came over and sat both drinks down. "There you go, JB," he said.

"Thanks." The barkeep turned away. "Wait a minute, Pinky." He turned back to face JB. "How do you know my name? Do I know you?"

It was a continuing source of amazement to JB that he could go almost anywhere in New York and run into someone he knew. Either it was a reflection on his social contacts or it meant New York was a smaller town than people gave it credit for. JB tended toward the latter.

The drag held out both arms as if he were playing a Christian martyr in a mystery play. "Do you mean to say that neither of you recognize me? I guess I shouldn't be surprised." He looked down at himself. "I have changed some." He looked back at JB and Len. "We all used to know each other. In fact, Len and I worked together. I didn't say anything before because I wanted to see if he remembered. He didn't."

Len peered at the bartender closely. But close inspection didn't help. There wasn't one single feature he recognized.

"And," the barkeep continued. "We were related when we did."

Len said, "You must have changed from Mr. Jekyll into Miss Hyde then because I have no idea who you are. What do you mean we were related? How? Fess up, sister man."

"Yes, please," JB said. "I don't remember ever in my entire life meeting Dame Edna's third cousin."

"It was a while ago. While you were still at the network."

Len shook his head. "Still not helping, dear."

"On your soap, Len. I'm an actor. Scott Trumbull. I played your dastardly nephew, Bartlett, for fifteen episodes."

Len had been the star of a Gothic soap opera several years before. It had made his career and made him a celebrity. It also dated back to the time when he and JB had first met each other.

Len said, "I remember that character, but he wasn't a drag queen. I would certainly remember any drag queens we might have had on the show. Although, I do have to admit the entire cast was made to dress pretty funny. Period, you know."

"I remember that story arc too," JB said. "Len, he was supposed to be a long lost relative and was plotting to get an inheritance or some such."

Scott nodded. "But Len's character pushed me off a paprpet to my death. That more or less ended my soap career at the same time."

"That could be just about any storyline we did on that show," Len explained. "Someone was always plotting against someone over something or some other. I'm sorry I killed you, but blame the writers. I just did what the script said."

Scott laughed. "Hey, that's showbiz. I survived. This bar gig isn't my main thing. I have my own theater company now."

"Well, that's cool."

"The Ridiculous Rhinoceros Company. Maybe you've heard of it? It's been doing okay."

"Which would explain the drag," JB said.

"Actually, I have heard of your group. In the gay rags. They profiled the company just a short while ago. You use drag as a political act, as an expression of outrage toward homophobia."

Scott threw his arms out and wiggled his chest. "Honey, when I shake these tits I wear it's always a political act. Besides, it's damn hard to ignore someone dressed like this."

"You have a point," Len said. "But why are you working as a bartender? It must be hell on your nails."

"The company has been getting some notice lately but it still doesn't pay the bills. This job does. And it provides me with a free room. I live upstairs, above this place. And the owners don't mind me working in drag." He patted the back of his head a-la Mae West "It gives the place some atmosphere. Ohhh."

JB said,"Plus, you get to answer people's questions about how you look and advertise your theater company at the same time. Very clever."

"There's purpose behind all this make-up." He picked up a towel and wiped at a glass. "So, are you two still together? After all this time?"

Len choked on his drink. "Good Lord , no. We would have slashed our wrists long ago if we were. Besides, JB snores."

"About all we can manage is being good friends, and sometimes even that can be strained to the limit. Snore, indeed. I don't..."

"Yes, you do, like a wounded wildebeast."

"I'll give you wounded, you..."

Scott interupted them. "Well, you sure sound like you two are still together. I've read about you in the papers, Len. On Broadway. That's fabu, girl. And you, JB. You're famous now too. Writing those mysteries. Is it true you solve the real cases and then fictionalize them for your books?"

"It's worked that way a couple of times, but I don't go out of my way looking for crimes to solve."

Footsteps on the stairs caused Len, JB, and Scott to look at who had entered. For Scott it was business. For JB and Len it was a gesture that happened whenever a gay bar door opened anywhere, sort of like a tinkling bell giving an angel his wings,

The man on the stairs waved and went to a stool at the far end of the bar. "Hey, Crystal, how about a draft?"

Scott nodded toward him and then turned back to face JB and Len. "That's me," he said. "My drag name in Crystal Van Ish. I'll be back in a sec." He walked over to the new arrival.

Len leaned over to JB. "So, do you remember him?"

"Vaguely. We all went out to dinner once, I think. As I remember he was talented but kind of blah. A wall-flower type."

"Not any more."

"True. So why have you dragged me—excuse the pun—down here this afternoon. I'm not usually a Village kind of guy, thank you very much."

"Cubby is upstairs right now talking to the owner. He's settling the details on the act. This is the club I'm going to be playing in. I thought you would like to see the showroom. It might spark some ideas for the act."

Scott had finished his tending duties and came back to stand with JB and Len.

"That guy just gave me some red-hot gossip. Want to hear?" He leaned in closer. "He told me the cops have found another body here in the Village. It's another of The Fairy Dust Killer victims."

"You mean the one in the water? I read about that one in the *Daily News*."

"No, this is another one. A second body just found today. Stuffed in a dumpster behind the Triangle bar. It's the same as the other one though. His genitals gone and his body painted that awful lilic color. That's two bodies this season. So far. And the season has only just begun. The cops had better catch this Fairy Dust nutjob soon or the Village is going to explode."

Chapter 4

The Fairy Dust Killer had been named that morbidly silly title by the New York media, not because of what one would suspect—that he went after gay men as his targets—but for the odd quirk he had of painting his victims a particular color of lilic before he dumped their bodies.

The color was a national brand house paint available in any local paint store, called Fairy Dust by some marketing genuis who earned his thirty-five thousand a year by coming up with the name for the manufactuer. It was a pale faded purple in tone and was totally bilious when applied to an entire wall. It was far too precious for anything other than a small child or one of Tennessee Williams' Southern women characters.

The Fairy Dust Killer had hit the papers big time the summer before when two mutilated naked bodies turned up painted that pale lilic color. The bodies had been found in the back lanes of the Village, so of course, the newspapers screamed in three-inch headlines that a killer was loose, not just in the area, but in the gay community. As if every New York gay person lived only within the confines of the West Village, like it was some sort of Warsaw Ghetto fenced in with gun turrets and guards marching it's perimeters.

Both of the victims had been tortured, whipped, and mutilated in the same fashion. Their genitalia had been cut away the same way the Ripper had his victims a hundred years before. That was crudely and hastily. And both of the men's bodies were entirely covered with the Fairy Dust paint color.

Those first two bodies were the only one's found last year, and as winter came upon the city, it looked as if the killer had gone underground, or had moved on, since no more bodies were found for the next several months. But, as this year's summer approched, the killer had become active again. The first body had been found just days ago in the water down by the piers, and now a second had been found behind one of the more popular bars along Christopher Street.

The first body had caused Village gay business owners and neighborhood leaders to demand that the police do something about catching the killer. And soon if not quicker. The business people knew that if he wasn't caught fast then their business' would suffer from the bad publicity. Most reasonable members of the gay population would abandon the area and spend their money in safer districts of the city.

Also chiming in were the more militant gay groups. They wanted the killer stopped because he represented one more bias hate crime in an atmosphere that was already far to accepting of such blatant homophobia.

The police were saying—hoping it was true— that since only two bodies were found last year the Fairy Dust Killer would stop at that number again this season. The militant gays, not believing the police, had threatened to form vigliante squads to guard the area and take care of him on their own.

And New York's daily papers had stridently, salaciously, drippingly trumpeted every tidbit the police had released and every gory detail from any dubious source that could be scrounged up. It was, at the least, a volatile situation for all concerned. The Village felt like a million eggshells waiting to be stepped on.

Cubby stuck his head out of the showroom door and beckoned Len and JB to come inside.

Before he followed after Len JB handed over a slip of paper to Scott. "Here's my number," JB told him. "Call me. I'd like to hear more about this theater company of yours. Maybe I can do something with you."

Sticking the paper into his bra, Scott said, "That would be great. I will."

Entering the showroom JB and Len turned their heads checking it out. Painted the same red as the outside room it was lit by ornate brass and crystal sconces that lined up along each wall. Theatrical spotlights hung on two bars suspended over the floor area, which served as the stage. Polished brass railings separated the stage from the circular banquette's with tables that rose in three tiers around the stage floor. It all had a theater-in-the-round appearance.

Cubby waved Len and JB to join him. He stood with another person, and seemed almost excited—at least one eyebrow was raised—as he said, "Didn't I tell you it was a great space, Len.

Perfect for your needs, right?"

"It's terrific, Cubby."

JB asked, "How many does it seat?"

The other person with Cubby, a blocky woman, said, "If the place is full to capacity we can sit about a hundred. That always depends on who's appearing, of course." The woman's voice, which she pitched to it's lower register, sounded as if she'd seen one too many Robert Mitchum movies.

Cubby played host. "This is Lezlee Barrett. She's the owner of the club. This is Jeremy Bent, the writer, and, you know Len Matthews."

They all shook hands. Len rubbed at his fingers after she let go. The woman had a very hardy grip. In fact, everything about this woman was hardy. She was, in the gay venacular, a dyke. A lesbian. And not of any lipstick variety either. She was a dyke with all the bull thrown in. She wore a man's shirt, blue jeans, and lumberjack boots. There had to be a tattoo on one bicep or the other.

She snorted a laugh. "The name really is Lezlee." She spelled it. "Mother had no idea how right she was gonna be when she named me. You can call me Lez. I like it better. Nice to meet you two. I'm looking forward to having you appear here, Len."

"It'll be fun." He turned in a circle. "Boy this room is so big. I didn't expect it to be so...well, grand."

"And people call me JB. Nice to meet you too.

"JB. So, Len, have you done cabaret before? We get a pretty interesting audience here."

Len's eyes crossed. "That translates to gay, picky, over-critical, and bitchy, right? Uh, Cubby, maybe this isn't such a good idea."

A sound coming from the top row of the banquettes caused them all to look up. A man was standing in the shadows up there. They could only make out his form, no features.

Lez held her hand up to cover her eyes. "Is that you Tom? It's okay. You can come down." She turned back to the three men. "That's my little brother. He does all the repair work here at the club. And he's the barboy at night." She said this with a degree of pride in her voice not usually associated with the position of maintenance worker.

"Thank God," Len said. "I thought maybe there was a Phantom of the Cabaret loose doing Lloyd Webber tunes. I can do without the competition, thank you very much." Len didn't get his expected reaction. Lez gave him a look that could wither a begonia.

Tom came into the light and down the steps to the stage. He was around thirty, dressed untidily in jeans and a stained T-strapped workout shirt. But the body underneath that shirt was nothing short of breathtaking. His wasn't a fashionable gym toned body with perfect symmetry and a light-bed tan, but muscled from hard work and heavy lifting. He was ripped and cut as if he was a piece of architecture. He was unshaven but still scruffily handsome, with soft brown puppy-dog eyes. Longish dark hair fell over his forehead constantly. His hand pushed it away, then again, and once again, and then again. It was a nervous tic, a serious convulsive action. He also walked with a limp, as if his one leg had a weight attached and he must drag it behind him.

When he had made his way down the steps and was a few feet away from the group he stopped. Lez went over to him to put a protective arm across his shoulder. This caused Tom to cringe and back away from her touch. She gently took one of his hands and pulled him closer to the group, but not without some hesitancy on his part. Then she introduced him.

He wasn't what anyone would call overly friendly or outgoing. Instead he seemed to be frightened of the three men standing in front of him. They were, after all, strangers to him. He wrapped his arms across his chest, hunching down to make himself as small as he could. With his bulk and muscles it was an impossible task but he gave it a try anyway. He nodded a greeting and asked them in a childlike voice, "Are you good men? We 've found out some men aren't. Are you?"

JB and Len looked at each other. JB said in what he hoped was a non-threatening tone, "I believe we are. Please don't be alarmed."

Tom seemed relieved at this. He nodded several times, then stood tall, stretching out of his huddle. He grinned sweetly. "That's good. Good," he almost sang.

He kept the smile but never really looked at them directly. It was painfully obvious that this handsome man had allowed himself to simply withdraw from his surroundings. He had moved way deep inside his head where he lived. It must have been a frightful place in there because he seemed afraid of everything around him, even a slight breeze.

Lez still held his hand tightly, guarding him like he was a new kid on the playground and she his appointed protector. She patted his hand. Then, as if talking to a child, she said, "These men..." She pointed to each of them in turn, "...are here to do a show. You'll be seeing them again."

Tom nodded and said, "Okay. That's good. If they are good men like thay said, then that's fine." He pulled his hand away from Lez. "Let go, sister, we have chores to do."

He moved away from the group and headed for the door. His hand returned to sweeping back his hair.

Len shook his head. "What a shame. Such a good looking boy." He asked Lez. "Is the condition from birth or..."

"Tom had a accident several years ago. He's been like that ever since."

"And you take care of him?," JB asked.

"I do. We're all we have. And thanks for not going all weird around him. Some people do."

"I just think it's sad. Poor guy," Len said.

"Actually, he's reasonably happy. So you don't need to worry yourself. Why don't we all go to the office and sign the papers. It's this way." Lez started to walk away'

Len, Cubby, and JB followed after her. "JB, it's strange," Len whispered. "I know that boy. From somewhere. I just can't remember where. But I will. Just give me time."

"Since your memory hasn't been at top strength of late don't burn out too many brain cells trying. And, please don't come up with it at four AM some morning. And if you do, for God's sake, keep it to yourself, you don't have to call me with the news."

Chapter 5

Cherries first floor office was actually more storeroom than business environment. Two desks over in a front corner was about the extent of anything office like. The rest of the space was a warren of boxes—boxes of booze, boxes of bottled beer, boxes and more boxes piled ceiling high filled the rest of the space. Standing against the far wall was a metal rack used for holding beer kegs. Next to that was a wire caged elevator shaft, and beside that was a two walled jerry-build plywood room with a door. This was built into the corner and was probably a smaller storeroom.

Lez led Len, Cubby, and JB over to the corner and the larger desk closest to the wall. At the other desk, set in front and to the side of Lez's, sat a small bleached out blond woman with large tearful eyes. She was pretty in a faded, wispy sort of way. Looking over a set of accounting books when they entered, she looked up, checked them out, and finding little in them of interest, went back to her books.

Lez took a seat behind her desk, opened a drawer and pulled out a cigarette and a matchbook. The cigarette was one of those extra millimeter. skinny, white-papered, gold-filtered, low-tarred, lite kind of smokes. A sissy cigarette that looked completely out of place hanging from where a blunt cigar would have been more at home.

"So, Cubby and I have worked out a nice little deal for you, Len." She struck a match and continued to talk while she lit her cigarette. "Seven shows each week. You'll have Monday's off." She waved at the cloud of smoke around her head from her first drag. "One show each week night at eleven-thirty, and two on Saturday. One on Sunday. You'll share in the take on a sixty-forty split, and we'll both share the PR duties and expenses. Does that sound good to you?"

JB said, "Eleven-thirty? Len. that's cutting it pretty close, isn't it? Can you get here in time after the play?"

No problem." Len said. "The Greenhouse curtain is usually down by ten-thirty. If I cut the bows short and leave my make-up on, I can cab down and be here in plenty of time."

"Sure," Cubby added. "I'll have everything already set up each night. All Len will have to do is grab a mic and be introduced."

"See. Easy as can be."

JB didn't look convinced

Cubby and Lez both tried to ease his concerns. Len, not concerned in the least, got up from his chair and went to the wall in back of Lez's desk. That wall was covered with hundreds of eight by ten headshots of the performers who had appeared downstairs in Cherries showroom.

The blond woman from the other desk got up and carrying the book she had been working on came around to stand beside Lez.

"Well, I suppose if the curtain is on time every night he can make it..."

Lez nodded, "Of course, and if he is held up Cubby will just vamp until he gets here. She turned to the woman, "Yes, babe, what is it?"

The woman spoke quietly, making an impression of a passive manner. It matched her pastel looks. "I need to show you this, Lez," she mewed.

"Okay, hon. Excuse me guys."

The woman laid the book down in front of Lez and they began to speak together in low voices as she pointed to a column.

JB got up from his chair and joined Len who was still looking at the pictures on the back wall. The pictures, held up with thumbtacks, were all of pretty looking people, posed as singles or in groups. Their names were printed at the bottom of each picture. Standard theatrical agents pictures.

"Quite a few current Broadway musical people here, JB."

"You'd know better than me, Len. You're the media maven in the group." JB spotted a picture that was placed slightly away from the rest, and was, unlike the others, kept in a black frame. The odd one out. It peaked JB's interest, so he stepped over, bent and looked closely at it.

It was another standard black and white studio shot of two men in their late teens. One was tall and thin and blond in the way only a California surfer dude could look. The other was not as tall, swarthier, stockier, and had longish dark colored hair. Both wore dark slacks and light colored sweaters, and they stood back to back looking out on what must have been a bright shiny world to them. The photo, from the lighting style and their clothing, looked as if it had been taken at least a decade before.

"Len, look at this."

Len came over and peered at the picture. "I'll be darned. I knew it."

Lez had finished her business and looked up again. "Guys, I'm not being very polite." She put her arm around the blond woman's waist. "This is DeDe. My wife." Lez said this, not in a loving affectionate way, but as if "wife" was DeDe's title. Like she was something Lez owned—a Ford maybe, or a new VCR.

DeDe nodded a curt hello, moved from Lez's grip, and went back to her desk. JB and Len returned to their chairs.

Len immediately pointed to the wall. "That picture over there. The one seperate from the others. It's of Tom and Timmy. The singing duo." He looked at JB and explained, "Like Desi and Dino." JB shook his head. "Okay, Peter and Gordon?" He still didn't get it. "Don't make me go back to the Boswell sisters."

He turned back to Lez. "Tom and Timmy were pretty big on the pop scene several years ago. They had a couple of top-forty hits and then stopped. They were really good too. What I think is interesting is that one of the two people in that picture looks very much like the man we met just a little while ago. Your brother. Is he..."

"Yeah. You got it," Lez admitted. "Tom was part of that act. But it was over way to soon. It was a case of hit it big, then poof, it was all gone. Such a shame."

Len went on. "The accident you mentioned downstairs. It was what finished the act, right. If I remember the gossip right, they were together and had a car accident. Timmy was killed, and Tom, obviousily, survived."

"And, if there is anybody on Earth that

knows about this sort of trivia it's going to be Len," JB added with a smirk.

Lez put a hand to her chin and pulled at a hair growing there. "The accident was terrible. Tom was driving and lost control of the car. Timmy died instantly they said. Tom broke his leg and his hip, several ribs, and had a major head injury from the steering wheel of the car. It took months and months for him to recover, if that's what you want to call it. Tom has been like you saw him downstairs ever since."

"And you became his guardian, so to speak."

"That's right. That's what big sisters do for their little brothers, right. We didn't know what to do at first. So we came East. Tom wanted to stay in the music business somehow, but I knew nothing about that. I did know how to pour a drink, so we bought this place with the insurance settlement, and combined the music with the bar. It's done all right."

"But, wasn't the accident out in California?" Len asked.

"You do know your trivia, don't you. That's right, but Tom wasn't happy out there. Too many memories, I guess, so we moved back here about nine years ago. That's when we took over this place."

"I get it. Cherries. *Cherry On Top* was Tom and Timmy's first big hit."

"Right. I was working as a gym teacher in the midwest when the accident happened. I didn't like teaching that much so I retired with a pension, got Tom better, and then we moved here to New York. As long as Tom keeps on his medication and this place brings in a little profit, we've managed to build a good life for ourselves."

JB said, "Medications?"

"Yeah, they keep him functioning. So he can work around here and stay connected. Without them he would just curl up into himself. He gets really withdrawn and won't come out of his room. It's like his whole life collapses." She paused for a moment. "But, what's wrong with Tom isn't your problem, is it? So, Len, do we have a deal or not?" She held up the contract.

JB said, "Len, before you sign you should ask about rehearsal time. Can you use the show-room? When will the space be available? For how long? That sort of thing."

"JB, you gigantic yenta, always looking out for me, aren't you?"

"Someone has to," he replied. "If left to your own devices you'd own the Triborough Bridge, and there isn't room for all that traffic in your apartment."

"DeDe handles the schedulling for the club," Lez said. "She can help you set up your rehearsal times."

"And we can use the Four-Two-Nine during the day if we need to," Cubby added. Lez nodded in agreement.

Len said, "Okay. That's handled, right?" He looked at JB. JB shrugged. "I'll sign."

Lez stood, shook Len's hand to seal the deal, and then, while offering her apologies, told them she had to leave for another meeting. After her goodbuys they turned to DeDe to set up the dates they would need the club.

Looking through her appointmtnt book she rattled off the available dates. Her manner now that Lez had gone was no longer quite so docile. Her tone was, in fact, downright hostile toward them. Len and Cubby conferred and picked their times. She noted them in her book and told them them they must be on time or suffer the consequences. Considering her manner they didn't dare ask what those might be. She finished with them and went back to her work.

On the way out Len looked back at her. "She doesn't like us very much, does she?"

"Maybe she's just busy," Cubby said.

"No, that's not it. She just doesn't like us. But everyone likes me. It must be you, JB."

"Me? What did I do? I didn't say boo to the woman. I nodded hello is all."

"That must be it. JB, you have an antagonistic nod."

Chapter 6

Staring at the blinking cursor on a computer screen waiting for the right word, any word, to pop into his mind was not the most constructive thing for a writer to be doing.

The ringing of the telephone then came as a welcome diversion for JB, who had been sitting in front of a blank screen for twenty minutes or so. Leaving the flashing accusatory cursor light he picked up the receiver. "Hello? Yes...Oh, Scott. How are you? This is a surprise. I expected to hear from you, but not so quickily. Its only been a couple of days. I'm not sure we can get together right away..."

Scott interrupted him. "JB, I know I asked you this before, but is it true that you get involved in the mystery cases you write about?"

"The police would probably prefer I didn't, but I have stuck my finger in a case or two. Why?"

"Can you come down here to my place? I have something here that might interest you. It's sure as hell a mystery."

"Well, I'm in the middle of...Ah, what the hell. Sure. But what is it?"

It's the damnedest thing I've ever seen. I'm at my apartment. Here at Cherries. I live up on the top floor. You go to the side of the building and take the stairs. See you."

JB hung up. Isn't this where Sherlock Holmes would say, *Ah-ha, the game is afoot?* But how can one resist somebody throwing down such a gauntlet? Or in Scott's case it would be a full-length opera glove, wouldn't it?

JB got his things and headed for the door, but stopped. Turning back, and feeling only the slightest twinge of guilt, he turned off the blinking cursor light.

At the back of Cherries JB found a set of skeletal, dirty, rusty looking stairs attached to the building by large henna colored bolts.

Never being particularly fond of either high places or rickety structures, JB prayed the stairs were steadier than they looked as he began to climb. Up a few steps he passed the perviousily visited first floor office, then he went carefully up to the second floor.

Once there he found a door colored with many layers and shades of paint. The current coat was a cheery lemon, but bits of red and blue, what looked like persimmon, and maybe some puce was showing where the yellow had chipped away.

He knocked.

In just a moment a radically different Scott than the one of a few days before opened the door. Minus his glitter drag Scott was nowhere near the same person. Thinly thatched white blond hair, heavy framed glasses, with a mockery of a chin on a pale complexion, he could have easily blended in at an albino convention, except for a pair of deep lapis eyes that stood out starkly from his skin. He reminded JB of a more healthy Andy Warhol.

This was the Scott JB remembered from back in the soap days. "Hi, guy. So what's this mystery you were telling me about?"

"Come on in. I'll show you." Scott turned and walked into the hallway leading to his front room. "I was cleaning out the back closet. And this thing was in the rear under a bunch of old clothes. I pulled it out thinking I could use it for a coffee table. But once I got it out here...Well, I decided to call you."

Scott pointed to a wooden trunk standing in the middle of the room. It wasn't much of a trunk, just a fairly large rectangle box made of old wood with dovetailed corners and a large black metal hasp on the front.

JB went over and quickly examined the outside. "Okay...So what's the mystery?"

"Inside, JB."

JB lifted the lid. "My God. Did you think to call the police?"

"No. I haven't. You were the first person I thought of when I saw that. I knew you'd be interested."

Inside the trunk, which was lined with old discolored tin, lying in a two inch depth of a tan and brown spotted powdery substance, was a bundle. It was shaped to form a letter N and covered in layer after layer of clear plastic kitchen wrap, as if it were a frozen rump roast. It was a human body. A completely wrapped hermetically sealed dead human body. Whether it was a man or a woman couldn't be distinguished because of the wrappings. But the stench coming off it clearly indicated the thing was once human.

"Whew. This is ripe. And you say it was in the closet? What the helll is a dead person doing in your closet?"

"A person? Are you sure? I thought it might be an animal. Some pet or something."

"I'm sure. Have you ever singed your eyebrows?" Scott nodded. "It's this smell, only this is times twelve. It's a person all right."

"Maybe we had better call the cops, JB."

"We will, but not right away. This body isn't new. It's been here at least a year. So the cops can wait for a while."

"How can you tell how old it it?"

"This powder in the bottom of the box. It's baking powder. There's an empty box there in the corner that has an expiration date of over a year ago. When did you move in here, Scott?"

"I didn't have anything to do with this. I moved in only a few months ago. I didn't even know that trunk was here until today."

"And you never smelled it?"

"No. It was all the way in the back of the closet at the back of the apartment under a pile of old clothes and stuff."

"And sealed in that tin lined box. When you opened it and exposed it to the air was when the smell got bad. And, whoever did this was concerned about that smell up to a year ago it looks like. All the plastic wrap didn't get rid of the smell completely, so he must have tried the baking poeder. Plus there were probably body fluids that needed soaking up. That explains why the powder is tan and not white.

Scott said, "Now that is completely gross." His pale skin went even paler and he went over to sit and fan his face with a hand.

"It's a completely natural part of body decomposition, Scott. What we need to figure out is why the body is here to begin with. And who put it here."

"This apartment had been empty for awhile before I moved in. And it was a mess when I did. That's why Lez let me have it rent free. I clean up the place and it isn't a squat for the neighborhood homeless anymore. So whoever did this could have been anyone."

"Have you got a pair of scissors?"

"Sure. What drag queen doesn't? Do you want pinking shears or just the regular kind?"

"Regular will do. Thanks."

He went to get them, and was back in seconds. JB took them and pinched a piece of the body's plastic covering at the head. He began to cut at the first layer, then the next.

"Is that a good idea JB?"

"It's the only way we;re going to find out anything about this body. Okay, this seems to be even older than I thought. Look."

JB held out a small cardboard tree. It was just one of many car air fresheners stuffed in between the layers of plastic.

"This is dated four years ago. And there's a bunch of them." He went back to his cutting. "Now, what's this? He held up a round object. It was discolored to a moldy green shade and was the size of a quarter. "It's a token of some kind. Made of brass."

"This is too weird, JB. It's like one of those English Christmas puddings. Full of little prize's and things. If you find a diamond ring its mine."

"Huh, now he's wrapped in black plastic instead of the clear. The killer must have started out using garbabge bags." JB again cut at the layers. A few more cuts and he uncovered the face.

"Jesus..." Scott turned away.

It was the face of what had been when alive a pale Caucasian young man. Strands of dry wispy blond hair hung over the man's still taut and unlined forehead. The eyes were sunk deeply into the skull. Bits of cheekbone were showing through where the skin had stretched and torn apart. The mouth was pulled back from a set of white teeth that looked too big for the cavity they were in. They were luminescent against the leathery dark tan color the skin had become over time. The face was thin and hollow cheeked. It was in the beginning stages of decomposition.

"The plastic wrapping kept the air from getting to the body. It's been kinda floating in it's own liquids all this time. That's what helped to preserve it. The skin is like a thin piece of cotton fabric. It would probably tear if I touch it."

"Don't. Don't touch it, JB. I'm already close to losing it. The smell is bad enough. Touch it and I hurl for sure."

"I won't. But now we know something about this poor guy. He's about twenty-five or thirty I would say. Doesn't look like he has any clothes on. He was a blond. And he was strangled. Look," he pointed to the neck. "There's the cord."

A length of torn lavender colored cloth was tied so tight it had sunk into the skin of the mummy's neck.

"I guess there isn't much else we can find out right now. Not without taking the body out of the trunk, and I don't think we want to do that. Okay, Scott, now we call the cops."

Just short of an hour later two plainclothes detectives arrived at Scott's apartment.

The one who did most of the talking, Detective DeAngelo by name, was in his late forties, dark featured and Italian looking. He was also overweight, fat on a frame not built for it. All the weight rode on his front, which gave him a stomach that protruded like a burl on a redwood tree. His suit was moderately expensive, well tailored, ecept it was done for thirty-five pounds ago. The coat fit nicely across the shoulders but wouldn't close over the belly. There was a wide field of stretched to button busting shirt showing. The pants were a U around his waist and under the stomach. Like many men who carry this kind of weight he had a perpetual film of sweat on his forehead. He wiped it away with an already damp handkerchief.

His partner was taller, younger, and in much better shape. He had a weightlifters body under a much less expensive suit. A testament to the pay scale of the NYPD. The seams of the coat strained across the broad shoulders and pumped chest. With dark red, almost brown colored wavy hair and piercing eyes, a firm jaw and full sensuous lips he would have been classified as hunk by any standard, gay or hetro.

Both men were standing in the living room checking out the wooden box and its contents.

DeAngelo asked, "Yoiu say you found this in a back closet. This morning?"

Scott said, "Yep. And I pulled it out here. When I saw that thing inside I called my friemd to come down here."

DeAngelo looked over at JB. "And who are

you anyway?"

"My name is Bent. Jeremy Bent."

Detective Peters, the hunkier of the two po-
licemen, wrote that information in his notebook.

DeAngelo picked up his questioning. "Okay,
Mr. Bend, you're the one who took it upon himself
to cut the plastic off the body?"

"That's Bent. Yes, I cut it open.'

"It's a pretty gruesome looking thing. It
didn't bother you? I mean the smell is pretty
bad."

"I've seen dead people before. Smelled them
too. I write murder mysteries, which means I do
a lot of research. Besides, at first we weren't even
sure it was a person in all that plastic. It could
have been a large animal. A doberman or something."

"Murder mysteries? Now I know you. I
heard about you from a colleague of mine. Kelly.
You know him? Lieutenant Kelly? Homicide?"

"Sure. He's a friend."

"That's not how he describes you. I think
pain in the ass were a couple of the words he
used."

Peters laughed. "Good one, Captain."

DeAngelo went on. "He said you have a way
of turning up in the middle of his cases."

"We've worked together a few times."

"Well, I won't have you getting in the middle
of my case. Understand?"

"Perfectly. Whatever you say..." JB stepped
back from the three men and went to sit on the
couch.

Now DeAngelo spoke again to Scott. "So,
you found this back there? In the closet."

Scott nodded.

"Check it out Peters. There might be something there." Peters went down the hall. "Now, what do you know about the body?"

Scott explained to the cop what he had told JB eariler.

"So, you opened the thing up, saw the wrapped mummy, and called Mr. Bend there. Why didn't you think to call us first?"

"It's like JB said. We weren't sure if it was a body...if it was an animal or something I wouldn't have any reason to call you guys. I would have called animal control."

"And you know nothing about this, huh?"

"That's right. I found it. Just like I said."

"When did you move into this place?"

"A few months ago. And that box didn't come with me. JB says it's got to be severeal years old. It was here way before I moved in."

"And how did you come to that conclusion, Mr. Bend?"

"It's Bent, with a T. It's because of the ex-piration date on the baking powder box...and on the trees. That's what convinced me. Oh, but I'm sorry, Detective. I'm not supposed to get involved, am I?"

"Expiriation dates?"

Scott showed him one of the air freshener trees and the box of powder. "There. That proves I didn't have anything to do with this."

"It doesn't prove anything really. So far it just means you had these things here. For how long is anyone's guess." DeAngelo bent down to gaze at the face of the dead man. "It looks as if he was strangled. There's a cord around his neck."

JB leaned toward the Detective. "Did you notice the color of the cord?"

"Yeah? So what?"

"It's lavender. Doesn't that mean something

to you?"

"What?"

"Well, since you've made it clear you don't want me interferring..."

"Listen, Bent with a T, don't be a smart ass. What are you getting at?"

"Isn't there a killer around that uses lavender as his calling card?"

"You mean the Fairy Dust guy?"

JB nodded.

"Can't be. This body doesn't fit the killers MO. This body isn't painted for one thing. He hasn't got the right color of hair for another. All the Fairy Dust vics have been dark haired. And this body is too old. The Fairy Dust Killer wasn't even around when this guy died, at least according to you and those expiration dates."

JB said, "Does it occur to you that this might be the beginning victim. That he's ground zero. The killers first. Serial killers evolve as they go along, right? This could be one of his earlier victims. It's just odd that this guy was strangled with that shade of purple cord. And that the killer is active in this area. Oh, but I'm sorry. I'm getting involved here and you don't want me to get the middle of your investigation, do you?"

"Do you have any idea how many murders happen in New York City during any given year? They number in the thousnads. That this poor guy, obviousily killed years ago, could be one of the Fairy Dust victims is way out there."

"None the less, I'll bet when you get all the plastic off this guy you'll find that his genitals are gone. That's another one of the Fairy Dust Killers little quirks, isn't it?"

"Yeah, well, we'll see."

Peter's returned from the hallway. "Captain, there wasn't anything back there that's incriminating. The closet's just got this guy's dresses and things in it."

"Dresses?"

"That's right, Captain. He's probably some sort of transvestite, or a transsexual, or something."

"Yeah?" DeAngelo turned to Scott. "Well, what sort of something are you?"

"Me? I'm just an ordinary guy who happens to look fabulous in sequins and chiffon."

JB tried to stifle a laugh.

"Not funny, mister."

"Really? I thought it was," Scott answered.

"You'd better watch it. We'll get the guys from the morgue here to pick this body up and get it out of here. I don't want you leaving town or anything. Peters, take their information. There are bound to be more questions that will need asking."

Chapter 7

Cubby, sitting in front of the grand piano in Cherries showroom, played the melody to Irving Berlin's song *I Love A Piano*. Len, standing in the curve of the instrument, sang out the words. On the twentieth bar of the song Cubby suddenly stopped playing, leaving Len with his arms out spread, songus interruptus.

"What's wrong? Did I hit a sour note?"

"No. You were fine. But I was thinking. You know what could be really funny for this song? For the show."

"Tell me."

"What if while you sang it you actually made love to the piano? Give the instrument a lusty, wanton, kind of seduction. Fondle it, feel it up, crawl all over it. I could be hilarious."

"That's a great idea. But why stop there. We could take it even further." Len lifted the lid on the piano. "What if I crawled inside the thing. I could disappear inside and make a bunch of sex sounds. Moans and stuff. He thought a moment.

"Or even better yet, we could play that Donna Summer record, *Love To Love Ya Baby*. With the sounds on that recording it would be a hoot. Once I was inside we could cut to the recording for a minute, then I would lift the lid, hang over the edge, pat the piano and ask if it was good for it too."

Cubby laughed. "It's sure something to work on. We would have to put a plywood shelf inside the piano though. Maybe Tom here at the club can help."

"You know, Cubby, it is a great idea and all, but one funny number doesn't make for a show. I'm going to need a bunch more material."

True. But isn't that what you have JB for? He's going to come up with a whole group of numbers."

"What kind of group?"

"It all depends on how you want to present yourself, Len. There are all kinds of acts, all kinds of performers. You know what we need to do? We need to get out and check out the scene. The entire cabaret circut. We need to find out what the audiences expect. Are you up for it?"

"You mean tonight? Well, sure, why not. But let me call JB and get him to come along too. If he's going to help write this act he'll need to see this too."

"Sure, we can make it a threesome. It'll be fun."

"God, I do love show-biz. Go out to night-clubs and call it work. And it's tax deductible."

All over Manhattan—from the East 60's to West 46th. From Madison Avenue down to Grove Street. From the Waldorf Astoria Hotel to the Village Vanguard. From Eighty-Eights to Don't Tell Mama's. The Five Oaks to the Fifty-Five Bar. From Danny's Skylite Room to the 92nd Street Y, cabaret is alive and serving its audiences.

Showing chanteuses and chansonniers showrooms flowered with talent. Julie Wilson with a single white gardinia in her hair. Margaret Whiting, Chita Rivera, and Dixie Carter all singing their respective hearts out.

Featuring musicians and mimics the rooms shimmered with excitement. Woody Allen playing jazz the way New Orleans does it. Michael Feinstein keeping the Gershwins music alive. Lipsinka and Lady Bunny, drag done with class. Bobby Short and Jennifer Holliday keeping Broadways lights lit.

Singers and dancers, actors and comics doing everything from vintage Sinatra to *Forbidden Broadway*. From a single singer standing alone in a spotlight to a Vegas style revue, there was something for every taste. From a lounge act to a full production it was all cabaret.

Len, JB and Cubby began early and finished late seeing acts, singers and revues. They sampled all of it, in all its versions. They found there were really no limits to what could be done as long as there was talent and sincerity, and maybe a bit of flash, to amuse.

At daybreak Cubby left the group at his apartment. JB and Len stayed in the cab, making sure he got inside. He weaved a bit doing so. All those drink minimums at all those clubs would do that to a person.

Then JB and Len continued on to their building, paid the driver, got inside JB's apartment, and flopped on his leather couch.

"I had no idea that fun could be this exhausting." Len flopped an arm over his eyes.

"Well, we certainly have a good idea of what's being presented out there now."

"So, do you have any idea's for my act?"

"You know, there's so much out there you could do. Just about anything and you'll get away with it. Puppet's doing origami if you want. Do you want to be Edith Piaf or Soupy Sales? It's completely up to you."

"Cubby said almost the same thing this afternoon. And I thought this was going to be easy. Just get up, sing a few songs, and get work in a musical."

JB sat up. "Crap. I've got to pee." He stood up and headed for the bathroom.

"You do that. And pee one for me. I'm too pooped." Len slipped out of his loafers and put his feet on the coffee table.

When JB came back he began removing the cash and coins from his pockets, including the token he had kept from Scott's place that morning. He dropped it all onto the table next to Len's feet.

"Do you want something, Len? Tell me now, because I don't think I'll get up again once I'm down."

"Coffee would be nice. One of those frothy, girl-talky kinds. You know the chocolate frappe razzel-berry half-decaf cappa crap-a-roonie kind."

"How about *Chock-Full-a-Nuts*?"

"Fine."

JB went to brew the coffee. Len leaned back and wiggled until he was comfortable. "So what should we do about all this?"

"With everything that's happened today I don't know where to start."

"I meant the act, JB."

"Nope. You've got to make your own decisions before I even begin."

"Okay. But like Scarlett I'll wait until some kind stranger comes by tomorrow. Or is that Blanche? Oh, well they are both Southern, so it don't matter a tick." He shrugged. "Why don't you tell me about that body in the trunk at Scott's. How weird was that?"

JB answered. "For any place else, pretty far out. For New York, no big deal. What I wonder about is why would whoever killed that guy want to keep the body? That's not exactly a brass Statue of Liberty or a I Heart NY T-shirt. Some souvenir, huh? But the really strange part was that cord around the mummies neck. It was lavender. The same color as this Fairy Dust Killer uses."

"But you said the body was old. It must have been there way before this Fairy Dust guy showed up killing people in the Village. And he doesn't keep them as souviners. There have been bodies scattered in nooks and crannies all over the Village so far."

"That's the same thing the Detective said when I brought it up." JB sat down a tray with two cups, a full pot of coffee, with a creamer, on the table in front of Len. "Maybe this Fairy Dust Killer is a sentimentilist and wanted to keep his first victim. Who can figure out a physco killer? Besides I think the detective is wrong. There is a connection betwen The Fairy Dust Killer and that mummy."

Len leaned forward and picked up his cup, poured it full from the pot, and took a sip. "And you told this officer that?"

"Sure. Why not?"

"Well, most cops don't like it pointed out to

them when they're wrong. Not the best way to get on his good side, JB."

"Not my job, Len. I'm the one that gets to bring up these sorts of questions, not sit passivily by and let the cops not take notice of an obvious connection."

Len picked up one of the coins that JB had thrown on the table minutes before. "JB, you sly puss. When did you get into porn?"

"What? What porn?"

"This." Len held out his hand. "This coin is a token from a sex arcade. You use these to start the loops in the booth at the porn store. You get five or six minutes of dirty movies for each token. I didn't know you went in for that sort of thing."

"I don't. Not very often anyway. That token was one of the coins wrapped in with the mummy. He was the dirty pictures kind of guy. Whoever he was." JB paused a moment. "Interesting," he said to no one in particular, then lapsed into silence.

"Oh, crap. I did it, didn't I, JB? This is a clue. And now you are going to look into it. Why do I keep getting you involved in these things? You're supposed to be working on my act, not running around after serial killers. Why do I keep doing this?"

JB looked up. "It's what a good sidekick is supposed to do, Len. Provide the necessary piece of the puzzle so the investigator can get on with the case. And I think you did it good this time. This token could be a major clue."

"But I don't want to play Watson to your Sherlock. I play the leading man, remember."

"Okay, then you get to be the other Hardy boy. I'm Joe and you're the one people wonder about."

Chapter 8

Opening his door, JB was pleasantly startled by who had rung his bell. "Well, good afternoon, Detective...uh, Peters, wasn't it? Is there something I can do for you?"

JB, who was standing in the doorway in his usual writing attire—an oversized T-shirt and red and green chili pepper silk boxers—was quite happy to find the attractive policeman at his apartment door. It had been several days before that he and Scott had called the cops about the mummy in Scott's apartment.

"That's right, Mr. Bent. It's Peters. I'm here at Captain DeAngelo's request..." JB caught the cop's eyes wandering over his body. Checking him out? Interesting. "...Uh, I'm supposed to ask you if you would please come down to the station for a talk?"

"Is this about the mummy? You've found out something, right?"

"I can't say, Mr. Bent. If you'll come with me Captain DeAngelo can fill you in at the station."

"Okay. But you have to call me JB If I do."

Since Detective Peters was standing in front of JB with a head full of rust colored hair and the kind of eyes that were known to make JB go all squiggly in the knees—and he was going so far as to actually be asking for his company—he could easily be convinced to follow this cop just about anywhere. "But let me get dressed first. Silk boxers are really only appropriate for a police questioning after five."

Peters said, "This isn't a formal interview anyway, uh, JB. That would require a sequin tie and a top hat." He smiled at his own comeback. JB smiled back.

"That's very good, Detective. Wait there, I'll be right back."

The ride down to the Village precinct house gave JB an opportunity for a bit of what he hoped was subtle flirting with the policeman.

Any man who could rise to the occasion with a funny remark as the detective had done before was going to generate some interest on JB's part. Wit always got his attention. And the fact the officer was beautiful didn't hurt either. So JB turned on the charm and sought out information about the officers likes and dislikes.

Not being sure if the detective was actually gay had caused JB to hold back on a full-out cruise on the guy. Straight men usually didn't consider it a compliment when they were cruised by gay people, although they should. And with twenty years of gay liberation affecting the style and manner of gay men everywhere it had become harder to figure out if one "walked the waterfront" as Tennessee Williams once described it.

Now-a-days there were gays who actually enjoyed sports, could throw a ball, didn't know chintz from shinola, and didn't even like Judy Garland. Living in the kind of world that accepted gays as human beings made it harder to discern if some homos were actually homo. The secret homosexual handshake had been forgotten, and the pinky decoder rings had been put away.

The end of the ride downtown came much too soon, with JB still no closer to figuring out the detective's proclivities. But whichever way Detective Peters leaned really had little importance when JB decided he just liked the guy. Friends might be better anyway. JB got out of the car, and while Peters parked the vehicle, he went into the station.

Following the directions given him by Peters he soon found Captain DeAngelo's office. When he opened the door he saw Scott sitting in one of the chairs in front of the officer's paper strewn desk. DeAngelo wasn't sitting in the seat on the other side.

JB said, "Scott? So they pulled you in on this too. How long have you been here?"

"Longer than I'm comfortable with. I don't like hanging around police stations. They make me nervous. A hangover from my mis-spent youth."

JB leaned over the desk and looked at the files scattered over it. Then he lifted the edge of one folder. He scanned the report inside. "I don't think we have to worry. They probably just want to check our story against what the forensics report tells them. They would have a preliminary report by now."

A shadow appeared at the frosted glass door. JB dropped the folder and took the seat next to Scott. Seconds later the door opened and Captain DeAngelo entered.

He was in shirtsleeves and suspenders, a blue and red striped tie curving over his belly. He carried a mug of coffee. Taking his seat he looked over his desktop and frowned. Somehow he could tell his mess had been disturbed. Picking up the exact folder JB had held he opened it, looked it over, and then looked up.

"Interesting reading isn't it, Mr. Bend."

"A reporter's curiosity, Captain. Sorry."

"Except you're a novelist, not a reporter."

JB smiled. "Even worse. I read it, then I make it up anyway."

"This is official information, you know?"

"I didn't have enough time to read very much, Captain. I got that it's an autopsy report, that's all. I'm sure no secrets have been breached. Now, if you'd like to leave the room again..."

"Well, that's not going to happen." DeAngelo leaned forward in his chair. "Let's just get into the meat of this, okay? I had you brought here to go over the information we've got so far. About your mummy."

Scott spoke up. "Not my mummy, Officer. You took it, you can keep it. Take it to parties, if you want."

"All right now," the cop warned him, then went on. "It looks like the mummy is at least five years old, more likely seven. So that should set your mind at ease. We can't be exactly sure how old the body is because of the condition it's in. But, it looks as if you couldn't have been involved since you didn't live on the premises at the time. Killers don't usually take a body all that far from the actual area they operate in."

'In fact, seven years ago I was touring. With

Cats. The first national tour. I wasn't even in New York then."

"So much the better for you."

JB asked, "You actually have found out something about the victim. Have you been able to identify him?"

"Yes, as a matter of fact, Bend, we have. Forensics was able to get a full set of fingerprints."

"Really? From a body in that state?"

"It wasn't so easy since the skin on the corpse was so fragile. They had to cut the hand off and soak it in a special resin solution to harden it before they could apply enough pressure to get the prints."

Scott swallowed hard. "Details aren't really necessary, Captain."

"From those prints we were able to identify the victim." DeAngelo checked the file in his hand. "His name was Thorenson. First name Jacob. He was a foreigner. Danish. Twenty-four years of age. Here on a student visa to NYU. He disappeared from his dorm seven and a half years ago and was never seen again. Happens every day in New York... people just up and vanish." DeAngelo shook his head at the foibles of New Yorkers. "Now, the guy was also a homosexual. The token...You did find some brass coins when you cut the mummy open, didn't you, Bend?" JB nodded. "Well, they were from a porn theater a few blocks from the building the body was found in. Named the Gayity. And our vic probably frequented the pickup places in the area too. We were able to go through his belongings. His dorm at the university had kept his things in storage. No one had claimed it. Anyway, there were gay newspapers and magazines, that sort of thing."

"So the vic picked up some rough trade here

in the Village and paid for it big time," JB said.

"That's what we figure. Some kinky scene with a stranger that went bad and he ended up in that trunk."

"What a shame. What about the lavender rope he was strangled with. Did you check on that?"

"You were right about one thing, Bend. The victim had been mutilated in the groin area. His penis had been removed. But that was all. The scrotum was still intact. That sort of mutilation doesn't fit the profile we have on The Fairy Dust Killer, so this body won't be considered one of his, no matter what you might think. There were several things that didn't fit the profile.

"Such as?"

"Such as..." amused cynicism shaded the Captains words, "First, the vic was a blond and fair skinned. The killer goes for dark hair and swathier types. And, the vic's body hadn't been whipped. The Killer is into sado-mascchistic type whipings. Also the vic's fingerprints were intact. The Killers vics all have their prints burnt off. We think that's done to make them harder to identify. And, most telling, the mummy still had his tongue. The Fairy Dust Killer's victims have all had their tongue's cut out."

"I didn't know about that. It hasn't been in the papers that the tongues were removed from the bodies."

"Bend, so far the department has had over ten people claiming to be The Fairy Dust Killer. We've kept some information back to use as a test."

"This profile you mentioned. It gives you a sort of picture of the killer, right?"

"Right. From other crimes and the set of

commonalities I mentioned we were able to work out a pretty good idea of what kind of person our killer is. For instance, the killer is presumed to be anywhere from his twenties to his late thirties. Most likely he's considered attractive, and he would probably be quite personable, the same way Ted Bundy was. If he wasn't the killer wouldn't be able to pick up his victims. He's probably from one of the boroughs since we have no reports of the paint being bought locally. And he's most likly a homophobe or hate-monger who is killing these men to rid the world of you homosexuals."

"Or to make something the victim has disappear, or to get revenge on someone, or too..."

"What's that, Bend?"

"Just thinking out loud, Captain. What exactly does your profile say about the paint and his choice of color?"

"That's obvious, isn't it. Lavender paint and lavender being the color most associated with the gays. The problem is the paint is a national brand and available everywhere. But we have flyers out so a purchase anywhere in the city of that color is reported immediately."

"Well, it sounds like you guys have been very busy. But, I don't know, Captain. That color thing is a pretty easy association. Too easy perhaps."

"Are you going to question a trained professional profilier, Bend?"

Uh, oh, maybe JB had gone to far? The Captain did seem inordinately proud of what his squad had come up with. Although it was all just a great big assumption on their part. "No, of course not. But it might be a good idea to dig a little deeper into the motives of this guy. It's just to pat."

"I'll pass that on, Bend. I'm sure our guy will love hearing your theory. Now, since neither of you seems to have any connection to the mummy, you can go. But there may be some more questions later. This is still an open case. Remember that."

"Yes, Captain."

The two men rose and headed for the door. JB turned back. "Oh, Captain, one more time. It's Bent not Bend."

"Whatever," the policman answered.

Chapter 9

Len, lying naked on the bed, stretched his arms above his head. He looked up just as Cubby, also naked, returned from the bathroom. Cubby sat on the bed, leaned over to Len and with a sly smile kissed him on the lips.

"Humm. Nice. I can't tell you how decadent I feel afterglowing in the middle of the afternoon. Delicious,"

"It might be afternoon to you, honey, but its the middle of the night for me. Remember I work evenings, Four AM is my eight AM.'

"Yes, Cubby, I know. I was with you at five this morning at *The Brassiere*. You were greeted like a long lost relative."

"I like an early breakfast, and the waitress there knows me. I tip her well."

"That's not the only thing you do well." Len traced his finger across Cubby's chest.

"Well, I can do that again..." Cubby leaned over and nuzzled at Len's neck. He smiled at the warm dampness of Cubby's mouth and the tickle of his tongue. He thought about how long it had been since anyone had made him feel like this. Cars had fins.

Len, for all his braggadocio, was quite aware he didn't have much of a social life. The acting career actually took up most of his time—chasing a career in the business of show could be totally life consuming. Besides there weren't many interesting men to be had in Cubby's and his age group—stage door Johns were out of Zigfield Follies tales of the twenties, and a bouncy twenty year old chorus boy with his latest gossip could be fun for a little while, but wasn't very intellectually stimulating in the long run. It had been such a pleasure to spend time with Cubby. They got to let their hair down and act their real ages for a change. It could be exhausting trying to stay hip all the time.

Just then Cubby ran his tongue across Len's chest. His focus shifted. Cubby had also been the tour director on the most amazing sexual excursion Len had been on since he couldn't remember when. Cars still had running boards and were called flivers.

Cubby's energy and enthusiasm for sex was astounding. He was indefatigable; ready to go again while Len was still wishing he had a cigarette. Cubby may have seemed laid back and dull in his everyday manner—which Len suspected had something to do with his visits two times a week with a shrink, and daily doses of Lithium, or Prozac, or Elivil, or some such—but lay the man out on a bed and he was a totally different person. Cloven hoofs and pan pipes came to mind.

Cubby then hummed into Len's belly button and he forgot to think altogether. He happily went with the feelings.

✤

JB and Scott came out of the police station and began to walk back through the Village together. They decided they were both hungry, so, being close, they decided to stop at the Tiffany Diner for their mid-afternoon meal.

The "Tiff" is a New York style Greek diner ideally located just off Sheridan Square and directly under the local muscle gym. This proximity afforded the diners a prime view as the buff muscled bods walked by on their way to pump up. Which was the main reason the restaurant existed. The food certainly wasn't reason enough.

Once JB and Scott were sitting in a booth by the window JB said, "Regardless of what DeAngelo and his high profile profiler thinks there is a connection to The Fairy Dust Killer in that mummy."

"Well, what can you do about it, JB?" Scott looked at the plastic covered menu quickly and told a passing waiter what he wanted.

JB did the same, then continued his thinking on the case, "What can I do? I intend to check out that porn place for one thing. What was the name again?"

"The Gayity. It's over on Houston. Just a few blocks from Cherries."

"Didn't DeAngelo say something about killers not going far to find their victims? That upstairs room...before you moved in...was a perfect place to take someone without being noticed. And its close enough to the porn shop the killer could get there unseen."

"Yeah. But with all the pick up spots to be had here in the Village it would be easy to find a victim just about anywhere..."

JB interrupted. "But the mummy had those tokens with it. Those were left for a reason I suspect. I read somewhere that serial killers, psychologically, want to be stopped. That's why they leave these kinds of clues behind, so they will be. Those tokens are just so blatant. There's no other choice but to go to this porn place,"

Scott said, "I'd go with you...I always enjoy a bit of the old nudge and tickle...but I have to work tonight." He looked at his watch. "And, if we don't get our food soon I'm going to be late. I still have to get dressed, and I have no idea what I'm going to wear."

"Ha. You sound like my little sister before she goes out on a date. Isn't the drag thing a real pain in the ass? Having to get all dolled up every-day?"

"It can be. But doing make-up as an actor in a play isn't any worse. And the upside is the Ridiculous Rhino Theater and what it does for the troup."

"Troup?"

"The Rhino has a core group...four of us... and we add people as we need for a particular show...and if we can find a theater."

"Your company is dark right now, isn't it? Is that because you don't have a theater?"

"Partly. We always have to rent a space to perform in, and that always costs. But I am working on our next show. A parody about Jayne Mansfield, as if she wasn't a parody to begin with. But it is down time that's rough on the company. I have Cherries, but the other three have to grab what they can. In fact, one of them, Trashy, will be playing piano tonight at Cherries."

"Trashy? The guy's name is Trashy?"

"We all have drag names, JB. They're better

known to the Village than our real ones. Mine is Crystal Van Ish. Then there's Trashy Slutcowsky, the delightful Vondalee Tiplicker, and, of course, Ophelia Longfellow.

"Of course..." JB rolled his eyes.

Scott again looked at his watch. "Do you think we can get our order to go? I am definately going to be late."

"Len. Len. Honey. It's time to wake up. There's just enough time for you to get dressed and get to the theater by seven." Cubby took hold of Len's hand as it swiped at his cheek. He leaned in and kissed Len on the neck. Len rubbed at his eyes and sat up. He swung a foot to the floor and headed to the bathroom.

Cubby followed and leaned in the doorway. "I was thinking. JB was worried about you getting down to the Village on time after your show. How about I meet you after curtain tonight and we test how long it takes? We could grab a cab, time it, and have a late supper when we get down there."

Len, more awake now, turned to face Cubby. "Great idea." He turned back to the sink where he spotted a powder residue on the glass shelf below the mirror. This powder residue was white—it could be talc—but was it? There was only one way to find out.

If it was what Len was thinking it was he could understand better where Cubby's energy had been coming from. What was it called? Oh, yeah, Peruvian marching powder. He wiped at the powder with his finger, and held the finger up as he turned to face Cubby again, Then, trying not to sound as judgemental as the words sounded in his head, he asked, "What's this?"

Scott opened the door, left the keys hanging in the lock, and headed for the bathroom.

From the hallway Scott said, "Make yourself comfortable, JB. I've got to get ready for work."

JB took the keys from the door. "You should be more careful with your keys, Scott. I'll put them here on the table."

Scott answered, "Sorry. But time isn't on my side here."

"That's true for all of us, buddy. From about the moment puberty hits we're all heading for midnight."

"Well, I'm supposed to be at six, and according to my watch, it's already nine."

JB went to the bathroom door and watched as Scott began to wash his face. "If it's so late how are you going to get dressed so fast? I was right, this drag thing is a pain in the ass."

"Lighten up, JB. I'v got a plan that will make it easy. I'll do a Cockette thing tonight. You remember them don't you. The guy's from San Francisco."

JB did remember them. A group of gay leather men that decided to twist gender identity by wearing full women's make-up with their leather drag. "Sure. Macho drag. Right?"

"Exactly. They screwed with everyone's gender expectations. The best part is to do the look I don't have to do any prep work. I don't even have to shave." Scott held up a small bottle. "Some glitter eyeshadow, a pair of eyelashes, some lipstick, and I'm done."

From the back of the apartment a voice called, "Scottie, are you here?"

Scott leaned over and looked out the bathroom door. "Yes, sweetie, I'm here," he called to the voice.

Tom, the club owner's brother, came limping down the hallway. He was in such a hurry he careened off one of the walls and almost lost his balance. He stopped a moment, took a breath, steadied himself, and then continued coming toward the bathroom. His face wore a worried expression and his eyes were filled with his habitual fear. His hand was pushing furiously at his hair.

He arrived at the door and immediately spoke to Scott. "Good, cause DeDe is in one of her moods. A real mean one this time." His head nodded vigorously. "Yes, it is, and...and it's scary, Scottie. Real scary." His agitation was such that he had not even noticed JB. "You know how she is when she's mad like this. She scares me. So hurry, please, Scotty." He shifted from one foot to the other.

JB asked, "What is it with DeDe anyway? She was out and out rude to Len and I the other day."

Tom turned to him. "Oh, hello, Mr. JB. She's not nice to anyone. No, she isn't. She doesn't like people very much. Except for Lez."

Scott generously applied a bright red lipstick to his mouth, then said, while a finger cleaned up the line, "DeDe just isn't nice to men. Doesn't like our sex. Individually or as a gender. At all. It stems from a really bad marraige. Some Latin guy that thought it was all right to abuse and beat on his woman. After she finally had enough of it she met Lez, who helped her get out of the whole mess. But DeDe does still hold a grudge against men in general."

Scott stopped applying his make-up and gave Tom a gentle look. "Don't worry, honey, I'll take care of her." He reached over and lightly rubbed Tom's hand with a finger. Tom immediately calmed and smiled brightly at Scott. For a quick moment his fear seemed almost gone. "Now, sweetie, do you know where my leather vest is?" Tom nodded. "Could you get it for me? Tom nodded again and headed for the living room.

"So you and Tom are an item?"

"More like best buds, really. But he is a terrific guy. And one hell of a cuddler. He and I have spent more than a few nights just holding on to each other. You have to admit that body of his is to die for. He's like a hard-muscled well-built stuffed animal. And he's not nearly as crazy as everyone thinks. His meds manage to keep him mostly on track."

JB said, "I haven't really thought of him as crazy. Just terribly injured from that accident he had. But what happens if he doesn't take those meds?"

"I really don't know. He been all right so far. He has said he's heard a voice lately. Talking to him." Scott leaned into the mirror and began applying the overlong eyelashes he would usually wear with his drag.

"It's no wonder he's so afraid all the time," JB said. "That would scare the shit out of me too. I wonder what the voice tells him?"

"He say's it's God. But, hell, a lot of people talk to God. I know I do. It's called praying. So how bad can it be?"

"That would depend on if Tom's God is peaceful and loving, doesn't it?"

Tom returned with Scott's vest and handed it over.

Scott wiggled into the garment without putting on a shirt, so the cleft of his pecs and the light fuzz of hair on his bare chest still showed. Then he snapped a silver studded armband on each bicep. He added a worn pair of cut-off button-fly jeans and then black leather chaps went over his legs. Heavy chain-swagged boots added a rough and ready touch to the costume. With glitter encrusted eyelids, two inch long eyelashes, blush red cheeks, and overpainted scarlet lips, plus a day's growth of beard stubble, he ended up looking effeminately clown like. A dark blond fake mustache glued under his nose seemed at once proper and out of place. Then a silver studded barracks black leather cap finished off the Castro-like retro look.

"Well?" Scott posed for JB.

"Get an Indian and a construction worker in here and singing Y-M-C-A would be perfect right about now."

Tom was standing in the doorway wringing his hands. His anxiety had returned. "Can we go, Scottie? DeDe will be so mad."

"Okay, Tom. Let's go. You coming JB?"

"Uh, no. I think I'll go to that other place."

"Right. Just lock the front door when you leave. Come to the bar when you finish. I'll buy you a drink."

"Scottie..."

"All right, Tom. See you later, JB."

JB nodded and went to the front door, leaving Scott and Tom to go downstairs and face the angry DeDe.

A bemused expression on his face, JB walked back toward Cherries from the porn theater he had left only moments before. As he approched the club he heard the muffled notes of a rinky-tink piano trying futilely to drown out a chorus of voices.

When he opened the door the louder sound from inside almost singed him, as if it were the blast of heat from an oven opened to check a cake for doneness.

Inside Cherries was packed to the proverbial tits with men standing shoulder to shoulder and five or six deep. With a median age somewhere in the late-forties to later fifties the group on the whole was graying, boisterous, over-styled, oversprayed, over-fussed, and trying way too hard to be attractive. They had all crowded around the club's upright piano, which was pounding out a tune from the Broadway show *Mame.*

The whole crowd happily sang along. However, this crowd wasn't pedestrian enough to just sing the melody. This one added all the chorus parts and harmonies too. A line of six guys over in the corner were doing a smaller version of the original Broadway chorus dance routine from the show.

JB smiled with sudden recogniation.

So that's what this place was all about, he realized. It was the oft-rumored and talked about—but seldom actually seen—chorus boy graveyard. Like the one for the African elephants Cherries was where old gay Broadway chorus boys went to die.

The piano segued into *Bring Him Home* from *Les Miz,* the English musical scheduled to open soon on Broadway. The crowd quieted as a haunting tenor voice rose above all the others to sing the melody—tenderly and longingly. JB stood on his toes to better see who the singer might be.

He stood beside the piano, a tray of dirty glasses in the crook of his arm. His eyes were closed as each note he sang transported him away from his troubled mind. His other hand was held out before him, for once not wipeing his hair out of his eyes. Tom's voice rose to capture and caress the haunting melody. Until he came to the last note which he held to then let fade softly away.

The crowd had listened with rapt attention and audibly sighed with pleasure at the last lingering note. Then they burst into applause. Tom flushed and skuttled back to his station.

Trashy Slutcowsky, the pianist, climbed up onto his bench and bellowed for quiet. Dressed as a cliche small-town piano teacher with a comic ample figure, tiny cupids-bow painted lips, a grey fingerwaved wig, glasses on a neck chain, and an Italian knit ladies suit he was a sight. The back of the skirt stretched tauntly across his bulldog in a sack rear end, and a ruffled lace blouse finished off the illusion with a perfectly fussy effect. Cuffs sticking out from the sleeves waved merrily as he told the crowd that up next was what they had been waiting for and could they keep it to a mild riot while he played.

He sat, prissily put on his glasses, peered at the sheet music before him, and then with appropriate glissandos began *Hello Dolly.* The crowd cheered and took up the song, again singing all the parts and harmonies.

JB laughed at the crowd's enthusiasim and noted the happy looks on each of their faces. Everyone, that is, except one person. One face sat alone at the bar, the look of abject misery giving the space it filled a Bette Davis bumpy night kind of feeling.

It was Len.

Chapter 10

It took him awhile but JB finally worked his way through the crowd and over to the bar. After much waving he managed to catch Scott's attention. He walked over to JB. JB pointed toward Len.

"Don't ask," Scott said. "I have no idea what's up with Mr. Morose. I've been way too busy to notice. When the bar gets like this there is no way I can focus on one single depressed fairy. But I did remove all the sharp objects that were around him a half-hour ago. I even moved the swizzle sticks."

"Thanks," JB said. "We wouldn't want him to swizz himself to death." Scott turned away intent on going back to work.

"You mean he's been here that long?" JB shouted after Scott.

He turned back. "He's been brooding like that all night. He makes Hamlet look like Chuckles the Clown. Talk to him, JB."

"But where? We can't talk here. It's too noisy and crowded for any kind of conversation."

Scott pointed to the showroom doorway. "Go in there." He held out the key. "You can use this." Scott looked toward the barboy station. "Now where the hell is Tom? I need another keg." He turned to face JB. "Help him, JB. Len probably just needs to talk."

"And once more I get to be his personal Wailing Wall. Oh, joy." JB went to stand behind Len. A glass filled with a clear liquid stood before him and his head was drooped like a starving petunia. JB tapped his shoulder. "Okay, Tiger-lily, pick up your drink, and your butt, and follow me."

"Len turned quickly. "JB, what are you doing here?"

"To hear why the suicide hotline has elected you tonight's poster boy. Come on, we can talk in there."

JB unlocked the showroom door and jerked his head toward the darkness of the room. Len, glass in hand, went through the door.

"First, dear God, tell me that glass isn't filled with booze...please."

JB flipped on the lights. There was a chill in the empty room. The air conditioner must have been set to its highest setting. Does it have to be this cold? It's cold enough to store meat. Maybe he should mention it to Lez, JB thought. But he realized she would only say that when the room was full of people, because of their body heat, it wouldn't be nearly so bad. But still cold enough to see your breath did seem excessive.

Len answered the question. "I'm bummed, JB, not bombed. It's just soda water."

"Good. Okay, what's wrong?"

Len sat at the piano. His finger picked out a note. A single note that hung in the air like a chime.

"It's Cubby."

"JB shook his head. "You're having man trouble? I don't believe it. You don't usually focus long enough on one man to have time for trouble."

"Well, this time it's different. I really like this guy."

Despite his surprise JB decided to take Len's declaration seriously. "So what's happened?"

"Cubby and I had an argument. I wanted him to stop using cocaine."

"In most groups that would seem like a reasonable request."

"That's what I thought." Len sighed. "Unfortunately, Cubby didn't agree. He started snorting the stuff this afternoon, and was still doing it six hours later when we got here after my show. He said he was doing it because it made him feel something. That he was tired of not feeling anything because of the pills he took."

"Pills?"

"Anti-depressants."

"So, that's what it was. That explains why he always walks around like he's one of the Addams Family. I knew there had to be a reason."

"Right. The pills were because he's been diagnosed as a manic-depressive. So he takes those pills. But at the least they come with a prescription. Coke doesn't."

JB walked over and sat next to Len at the piano. "And the prescribed pills are supposed to keep him on an even keel," he said. "No more major ups, and no more just as major downs. I suppose there's no problem losing the downs, but I'll bet he really misses the highs. He needs them like a junkie needs herion. Manic-depressives can be the same as addicts needing their drugs. They crave those highs."

Len looked surprised. "That's what Cubby said. How did you know?"

"It's classic," JB answered. "Right out of page forty-four of the textbook. So, by doing the coke he get some of his edge back. It makes him feel like he's alive again."

Len nodded. "But, JB, he's been doing so much of the stuff. And not just today. I finally realized that he's been on that stuff for weeks now. I know I said I didn't care what he did, but I do. It bothers me."

"Len, I'm really glad to hear that. It means you're finally starting to take being sober seriously."

"I just can't stand seeing him doing that junk. He gets crazy. He looks at me with these wide-open eyes. But they're just dead inside. They stare at me, as if somehow I should be able to fill them. It's really hard to deal with. I don't like being around him when he's like that."

"So you confronted him. And when you asked him to stop he left. That's not a surprise, Len. It's what addicts do. The high becomes more important than any person does. You even did it once. To me."

Len took JB's hand. "And now I know how you felt, JB. I'm so sorry."

"It was awhile ago. I'm mostly over it. You know, Len, hanging out with someone who uses, whether they use booze or drugs, isn't the smartest thing now that you're sober."

"I know you don't like Cubby, JB. I think you made that pretty obvious from the start. But I do like him. More than I care to admit. Regardless of his drugging."

"Len, I've never said I don't like Cubby.

What I actually think is that since he uses both alcohol and drugs he's not the best person for an addict...like you are...to become involved with. He might be a lot of things, even a knight on a white charger, but he also offers a whole range of temptations that are not in your best interests. I hate to say it, but this break-up is probably for the best."

"JB, there are times when you are truly a monumental prig. Especially right now." Len realized what he'd said and backpeddled. "I'm sorry, JB, even I know you're right. Okay, I shouldn't be seeing Cubby. He's bad for me. But that doesn't stop me from wanting him. And it doesn't make his not being here any easier to deal with."

"Len, I have to admit I honestly didn't realize he meant so much to you."

"Well, he does. And I don't like that I can't see him."

JB reached over and put his arms around his friend. He pulled him close.

"You'll feel better about this when a little time passes, Len. I promise."

Len broke away and turned again to the piano. He once again hit a single key. It was lower this time and sadder somehow.

"JB, you know there's another problem here. If Cubby isn't around what am I going to do for an accompanist?"

Len held his hands outspread over the piano and let them fall. They hit on several keys, striking a cacophony of chords.

"So, JB, have you thought about that? Well, I have. I still don't have a full act. Cubby and I have only worked out a couple of bits so far. And time is running out. Opening night for this cabaret thing is only a week away. Cubby was supposed to help put this together."

"And you signed a contract, so you can't get out of it, can you? Not without it costing you a whole lot of money. We'll just have to come up with something else."

"But what?" It's not like we have a whole company of actors like up on Broadway. This is just me, JB. All alone on a stage. With what? A pantomime act, maybe? Do you have a record player and a copy of *Judy At Carnegie Hall*?"

JB sat staring at the piano for a moment thinking. Then he reached out and struck a C sharp. It vibrated then faded. "No, no record player, but I do know where we can find a company of out of work drag queens."

"What the hell are you talking about?"

"Scott. That's who."

"The bartender?"

"No, Scott, or should I say, Crystal Van Ish and the Ridiculous Rhinoceros Theater Company. Which just happens to include a queen called Trashy Slutkowsky. Who plays a mean piano by the way. Put it all together, and I bet we could come up with one hell of an act."

"Impossible." Len shook his head.

"What's your better idea?"

"Trashy does play a hell of a showtune."

"I thought so."

"Do you think they'll do it?"

"Scott said the company was dark right now. And if they were in for a piece of the action..."

"How big a piece?," Len asked.

"Whatever it takes to get them to do it, Len. We have very few options at this point."

"Okay. Okay. I just would just like to make back my expenses, all right?"

"Actually if this idea works out the way I think it could, you'll make a lot more than that. I say we talk to Scott tomorrow."

"Tomorrow? He's right outside. Just the other side of that door. What's wrong with now?"

"Because I have to get to work."

"Excuse me, did you say work?"

"That's right. I have a job."

"Since when?"

"An hour ago. I went to that porn place..."

Len interrupted incredulously, "And now you work there?"

"Well, they weren't very forthcoming with answers to my questions. In fact, the clerk practically threw me out the door. But when I was leaving I spotted a sign about them needing help. So..."

"So, you asked for a job..."

"I spoke to the manager, not the clerk."

Len smirked. "And you were hired?"

"For the graveyard shift. I start tonight."

Len started to laugh.

"What's so funny?"

"That little old porn monger...you!" He started to laugh again. Then he stopped. "Say, do you think you can get me a discount?"

Chapter 11

Brian, the porn store manager, waved to JB from behind the Plexiglas enclosure that protected the counter and the cash register. He came over and opened both the top and bottom of a Dutch door to let JB step up onto the deck that overlooked the entire store. The clock on the wall had it at eleven-forty-five.

Surprise in his voice, Brian said, "You showed up. Great. A lot of new hires don't. They start thinking about how they're going to tell their families they're selling porn."

"No problem," JB answered"For one thing it doesn't bother me to sell this stuff. It's a product, basically the same as a washing machine, and people want those."

"True, and believe me, they want this stuff too. Porn has become a million dollar a year indutry."

"That's what I mean. Besides my family lives in the Midwest."

Brian laughed. He was thirty but looked

older. He had the look that JB had seen too many times these last few years. He was thin, too thin, skeleton thin, and appeared even more so because he wore a sharply ironed standard cut shirt that bunched in loose folds on his slight frame. His eyes, filled with humor, looked from a face with a bone sharp jawline. His skin was matte toned, flesh but with no life behind it. It was as if his life force had been sucked into his very core, necessary there just to keep him going. He was what the AIDS community was calling a long-term survivor in an atmosphere where 'long" could be only a week or a month.

"Why don't you look around and check out the merchandise," he said. "I'll be with you in a moment."

JB stepped down onto the speckeled black vinyl floor. Vinyl, he was thinking, because it was easy to keep clean and it was cheap. The store's walls were colored a yellowing white with what was once red—and was now a dung brown—trim.

On the walls facing JB, protected behind clear Plexiglas panels with locks, was a startlingly large variety of sex-toys. Everything from a pinky finger sized vibrator to a two foot long double-headed dildo. There were blow-up dolls, male and female, with and without real hair, all with the requisite openings. Next to those were latex vaginas, again with and without hair. Then came molded cocks in various sizes, although large dominated. Next were several different penis enlargement devices. Along side those were groups of lubricants and flavored oils, then came rows of condoms. These featured ribs and reservoirs, came in shapes, and with attachments on the tips to give the user an "extra feeling".

Another whole section was devoted strictly

to leather goods. There were whips in all lengths, and cockrings in all sizes. Black zippered hoods, some with silver studs and spikes, some with metal rings and leather ties. Enough cowhide was displayed to make just about any S&Mer cum in his black studded leather jock.

On the other walls were wire shelves holding plastic wrapped magazines, paperbacks, and hundreds of videos. Each video type was seperated by signs above describing the combination to be found below—boy/girl, girl/girl, boy/boy, Bi-sexual, S&M, B&D, A&P. Your choice.

JB picked up one of the video boxes. It was empty. The films must have been kept behind the enclosed counter. As if verifying his assumption Brian came up behind him and said, "They're empty to stop the shoplifting. It's a real problem. They even break the locks to get to the stuff."

"Really? Okay, listen, I'll tell you right away that if I see anything being stolen I'm not going to try to stop them. People in this town are too crazy and I'm not going to put my life in danger over a couple pounds of latex. If they want a dildo that badly, they can have it."

"I get it. It's not a problem. In fact, it's what I would expect. That's why the counter is glassed in. For your protection. Come on, I'll show you the rest of the place."

Brian headed toward a double door sized opening on the back wall. All that could be seen from out front was a lighted showcase that held boxes of porn tapes arranged in rows. Each box had a number under it. Blocking the doorway, preventing easy entrance to whatever lay behind, was a subway type turnstile. Brian patted the turnstile. "This is controlled by you with a button by the register. Each customer has to be buzzed in. After they pay, of course."

"What's that?"

"I said after they pay..."

"That's what I meant. What do they pay?"

"Oh. The entrance charge is six bucks. That's good for all night, with no in and out privileges. Unless the in and out is kept inside there."

Brian leered humorously and pointed to beyond the turnstile. With a key he released the device so they could go through. On the hall floor were painted orange glow-in-the-dark footprints leading off into the darkness.

"Let your eyes get used to the dark, then we'll go on."

JB moved aweay from the light of the lobby and leaned next to a dark tinted window with a change slot at the bottom. It had been cut into the wall and looked in on the register section of the store.

Brian came up beside him.

"Okay, what's in there?" JB pointed toward the darkness.

"Come on, I'll show you."

JB followed him and stepped around the partition into the side aisle of a small movie theater—six rows of seats back from a large screen with a TV video projected screen image. Currently it was showing two men tearing off each other's clothes in preperation for the sex to come.

Seated in the rows were ten or so dark shapes, presumably men, each sunk down and barely visible above the backs of the seats, staring at the fuzzy out of focus picture on the screen.

The theater was completly silent with only the sound of the men's occasionally shuffling bodies to indicate actual people were watching.

The video's pounding musical suto-hip score was abetted by a hollow soundtrack of looped dirty words and fake heavy breathing. There was a back odor of sweat, piss, and poppers which gave the place a sexual blatancy that was heavy and palpable. The viewers were in that same condition.

Brian leaned over and whispered, "We run gay porn only. No straight stuff, although we do sell it. But nobody want to see it here. You change the video's up front. And you sell tokens through the window back there."

"Tokens? What are they for?"

"Come on." Brian walked down the aisle to a curtained doorway leading to the area behind the screen. He held it open for JB to enter.

JB found himself in another dimly lit hallway, off of which were two shorter hallways. These short halls were made up of closet like numbered booths facing each other on each side. Each booth had a small red light bulb above its door. Some of the bulbs were lit—many were not. Many of the booth doors were closed—some were not. Inside the open doors were four by four spaces with a television screen and a multi-channel token slot situated on the back wall. The sixteen inch screens were there to show clips from the video's JB had seen advertised at the front. Also, inside the rooms, at crotch height, were fist sized holes roughly cut into the plywood partitions. These gave access to the next booth and whoever might be standing there. Glory holes.

Between the booth doors several men were leaning, trying to look as casual as possible. Each was affecting an attitude laden and predatory pose. Each was ready to strike should an attractive enough man walk past. It reminded JB of boa constrictors hanging in jungle trees ready to drop on unsuspecting victims.

Inside the open booth doors stood other men. Each was presenting themselves for view. Some were cupping bulging crotches, some openly fondled themselves. All of them were there for the inspection of other men walking up and down the halls checking out the merchandise on display. JB quickly realized what the place really was—it was a sexual showcase. Porn was only a secondary product to the store's main purpose as an indoor meet/meat rack and butcher shop. The booths were used to test the men's goods. To decide if they were USDA choice or plain ground beef. It was sex as product. Madison Avenue would love this place.

Suddenly the men along the aisle snapped to attention and looked wildly around. Fear was plain on their faces. Was there a raid? They were reacting to the blast of a siren that had blatantly disturbed the funereal quiet of the place.

"Damn," Brian said. "This happens at least once every night." He had to shout to be heard over the wail of the siren. "Some jerkwad always opens that damned backdoor."

Brian headed off toward the back of the building, JB went after him. The men along the aisle stood aside, but JB could still feel the men's eyes checking, watching, scanning, judging him as he passed them.

At the end of the aisle was an open space lit only by the red of an exit sign set high on the back wall.

Black painted plywood platforms of various heights were set in a half circle around the edges of this space. Customers used this darkened area for resting weary feet, smoking cigarettes, for surreptitious joints, and for the occasional group orgy.

Brian walked behind one of the taller platforms and got out his set of keys. He inserted the key into a blacked out glass and aluminum door located there. He turned the key, then, with some effort, lifted and reset the bar that stretched across the door. The wailing stopped, quiet was restored, and he removed the key.

"We have to keep this door unlocked because of the Fire Marshall. So we hide it back here behind the platforms and try to discourage people with the siren. But, there's always some asshole too lazy to walk to the front who tries to get out this way. Usually the bar on the door is so stiff that they can't get it open, but then some musclehead has to prove he's Hercules and sets off the alarm. If it happens you'll have to come back and turn it off with this key."

Brian took JB back to the front of the store. There were three men at the counter waiting to get in. JB, once Brian opened the door to inside the booth, took their money, put it in the drawer, found the turnstile button, and buzzed them in. He turned back to Brian.

"You catch on quick," Brian said. "So, that's about it. Collect the money, sell tokens through the window, and try to stay awake. Bring something to read if you want. Your relief comes in at seven in the morning. The place isn't really all that busy except on the weekends. That's when you'll be on the schedule." Brian went toward the office door. "Oh, the cleaning crew comes in at six. But if anything happens in the back before then you'll have to get it. And drunks do throw up. I'll be up and can let the crew in tomorrow." He pointed to an area above the register. "And notice the cameras. They'll see everything that goes on out here. We used to have cameras in the back, but they got stolen the first night they were up. The wires are still hanging back there. Also, notice the cameras are focused on what you do, not on the customers. If there's a discrepancy in the cash or anything is missing that video will cover your ass. Think you can handle it?"

"It doesn't seem that hard. Sure."

"Great. Then I'm going to get some sleep. Wake me if you need me. I'll stay here for your first night. It's good to have you here."

Brian disappeared into the office and JB was left on his own. After buzzing in the next ten or so customers, looking through the open porn magazines next to the register, buzzing in more customers, selling bottles of faux poppers, ex-changing bills for tokens, changing videos, and ringing up his first dildo—by four-thirty AM it had slowed to a snails pace and JB could barely keep his eyes open. And throughout the night not even one particularly suspicious or criminal type had come in. Only the regular horny Christopher Street types.

Then, at five AM, at the register stood a man who every detective from Holmes to Hammett would think of as suspicious looking. JB quickly made the same assessmant. This one was surely up to something.

He was tall and dark with a truckdrivers build. He was wearing a dark navy peacoat. Suspicious since it was almost summer and it was warm out.

On his head was a slouch of a hat pulled down to cover his eyes. Also suspicious.

A day's growth of heavy beard followed along a hard edged jaw and around a cruel slit of a mouth.

This guy could be the one, JB was thinking. He's big enough and mean looking enough to intimidate most anyone. JB took the man's money and handed over the tokens he'd requested. Well, well. That puts him in the booths. It would be easy for him to catch some unsuspecting guy in one of those booths. I need to keep an eye on this one.

JB changed his mind when the bruiser left the cage and walked to the turnstile. Sticking out from under his peacoat was a set of nylon stocking covered legs ending in a pair of three inch platform high-heels with rafia daisies as decoration at the toes. Hard to catch or carry someone in that getup, JB decided.

After buzzing the trucker/drag in JB was left to wonder—You'd think the guy would hate ruining the knees of his nylons on the hard tile floors of the booths, wouldn't you?

The shift dragged on toward morning.

Chapter 12

The three men were crowded in front of Scott, who was standing behind the bar holding a newspaper. He read from a front page article.

"This body, the third of The Fairy Dust Killer's victims this year, was found Saturday morning, mangled and badly mutilated. He was also painted the usual shade of lilac..." Scott stopped speaking and read silently.

"We can't read your mind, dear. What little of it there is. Outloud please."

Scott looked up. "Oh, sorry, Ophelia. Let's see...'the body was found beside the steps of the meeting rooms of the church at Christopher and Sixth Ave.'..."

"That's right across the street from Bras and Girdles right?"

"...'at seven AM this morning. The church maintenance man discovered the body. Thinking it was a homeless person huddled on the steps for warmth he touched it to wake it. At that touch the body fell over, the trash bag it was wrapped in opened and its purple painted arm fell out'...'

"Jesus."

"That's probably what the janitor said. What I want to know is how could this Fairy Dust guy dump a body there? Of all places. There's always people around that church. It's just off Sixth, for crips sake."

One of the three said, "There aren't a lot of people out really early. When its still dark. When was the last time you were up before ten on a Saturday morning, queen?"

And the other added. "Besides, who's going to notice a dirty old hunched over tramp all dressed in black limping along Christopher with a garbage bag over his shoulder..."

All of the men looked at the speaker.

He hesitated but then continued. "...or say anything to anybody if they did...even if they might have seen such a thing...which they didn't..."

The man closest to him reached over and grabbed a piece of the speaker's shirt. "Girl, are you just gussin' here? Or did you actually see something?"

The other man moved behind the speaker and took hold of his shoulders to shake him. "You never could keep a secret, dearie. What's this about?"

The man in front leaned toward the captive. "You better talk, queen."

Scott, from his place behind the bar, said. "You may as well tell, VondaLee. So far you're doing a lousy job of keeping it to yourself. Trashy's right...while being his usual overly dramatic self... if you know something you've got to tell..."

The front door opened, effectively putting a halt to VondaLee's unwilling confession. The three men, still in their interrogatory pose, watched as

JB and Len decended the stairs. They walked over to the bar, sat, and said hello to Scott.

Scott responded with a wave and then introduced JB and Len to the three other members of the Rhinoceros troupe. Ophelia behind, Trashy in front, and VondaLee caught in the middle.

Each of the three men in regular everyday clothing might have been taken for college students or young business types. The only indication that they did drag was a conspicuous lack of eyebrows. To make applying make-up easier they had all shaved their natural brows. It gave them a look of constant surprise.

"Nice to meet you guys. I'm not interrupting some ritual here, am I?"

Scott said. "No. No. They're just playing." The men all took seats along the bar. "Well, everyone is here, JB. So what did you want us for?"

"In a moment. Right now I need coffee. Please. I'm not even awake. My brain is refusing to function."

Len explained. "He started a graveyard job last night. He's not used to the sleep patterns yet...or the lack thereof."

VondaLee said. "Welcome to the land of the living dead. You'll eventually get used to the hours, but you are now a member of the permanently sleep deprived. It does make for some rather nice hullucinations though. Better than drugs even."

Trashy said, "Is that what you had this morning, VondaLee? Thinking you saw The Fairy Dust Killer?"

"Humm, you know that could explain it."

"The fact that that you're an overage, dumpy, silly ass queen would explain it too."

VondaLee sat up straight. "Dumpy? What's that mean? I've lost three pounds in the last week."

"Yeah. All of them from between your ears."

JB took a sip from the coffee Scott had brought over. He turned the newspaper lying on the bar around so he could read it, and noticed the headline. He then quickly skimmed the story and fell naturally into his Sam Spade ace detective questioning mode. He asked, "Would explain what, VondaLee? Did you see something that relates to this story?" He tapped on the newspaper. "To the latest Fairy Dust killing?"

"Not really. I mean, I was on Christopher early this morning and spotted a homeless man going toward the church with a garbage bag over his shoulder. That's all."

Trashy threw up his arms. "That's all! Queen, that was him. You saw The Fairy Dust Killer himself!"

"Come on, Trashy. It could have been anyone," Ophelia said, being the voice of reason. "It isn't unusual to see a homeless person on Christopher...even one carrying a garbage bag,"

JB shook his head. "But, put together with the location of the killers latest body...it might have some bearing. What did this person you saw look like, VondaLee?"

"Well, I couldn't actually see him. Up close I mean. I was at least a block away."

"Then you aren't sure of what it was?"

"That's what I've been trying to say. All I saw was a figure hunched over and walking on the dark street all dressed in black. Even the garbage bag was black. I wasn't close enough for any details."

JB asked. "Could you tell if the man was old or young? Tall? Short? A man even? A big woman, maybe? Anything that would make it stand out?"

"I'm sorry. No."

"Then what good are you?" Trashy reached over and slapped him on the back of the neck.

"Ow! That hurt." VondaLee raised his hand and slapped toward Trashy, who ducked, so that VondaLee connected with Ophelia's arm.

"Don't start with me, queen." Ophelia rose from his stool and leaned toward VondaLee with his hand raised.

Scott broke in. "That's enough, guys. All that's missing here is a stripper and a set of drums and we could revive burlesque."

Len added, "Or a Three Stooges routine."

The men settled down. Scott turned to JB. "So, what VondaLee saw really won't help, right?" JB nodded. "Then can we move on to the reason you got us here?"

Len spoke up. "Yes, please. I'm between shows here and don't have time for futzing around."

"Right," JB said. "You do have an evening performance don't you? When do you have to be there?"

Len's tone was peevish. "In about five hours. So let's get on with it, JB."

"You know, Len, I could easily leave you hanging in the wind all by yourself here. This isn't my problem."

Len pulled back his hand preparing to hit at JB. "I'll make it your prob..."

Trashy lookd from one to the other. "So what is this? A two stooges routine?" He smiled maliciously.

Scott said, "So, what is the problem, JB?"

JB went on to explain the trouble Len had

been having getting his act together for Cherries showroom and how close the openiing date was. He finished by saying, "So what I'm suggesting is that your troupe and Len work together. How about it? You said the group was dark right now. This would get you back on the boards."

Len added, "And since I don't expect you to work for free I would make sure each of you gets a cut of the nightly house. A cut of my cut that is. That's money. Maybe not a lot, but money."

Scott and the rest perked up. "Len, you just said the magic word. You now have our total attention."

"Great." Len went on enthusiasticly, selling his idea. "What we'll have to do is come up with at least forty-five minutes of material...possibly more if it goes over well. Songs, monologues, routines, stuff like that. Something more interesting than me standing there changing oxygen to carbon dioxide."

JB said, "Scott, what you said a minute ago isn't such an awful idea. Why couldn't we do a burlesque revival?"

"Because," Scott answered, "its been done to death. If I see one more production of *Sugar Babies* I'll barf, I swear I will."

"Okay. Scratch that suggestion. We'll do something else."

Len spoke, "We could keep it simple. I have a couple of numbers so far. Why don't each of you do one or two of your own routines. That would fill the time. And, as you all know, forty-five minutes can be a lifetime when you're standing in front of an audience."

Trashy said, "Not bad, but we would have to make some sense of all of us being together on the billing. We should do some bits as a group too. I have a song I've been working on. It's called *I've Got Those Suck The Blood From Your Neck Because I'm A Vampire Blues.* Len could do the lead dressed as Dracula with Ophelia and Von-daLee doing doo-wop backup as Frankenstein's brides."

"That would be great."

"Trashy," Ophelia said, "why don't we do the Christmas thing. Where we end up decorating Len? It's a cute number."

"Sure, why not? We all sing *We Need A Little Christmas* and hang tensil and decorations off you."

Len did a classic double take. "And just what is the tinsel being hung off of, if I may ask?"

"Anything sticking out," VondaLee said. They all laughed.

Scott asked, "We're still stuck for a name. What are we going to call this?"

Len leaned his chin on a fist. "Considering that last remark, how about a sex circus?"

Ophelia piped up. "In the old days this would have been called a vaudeville."

"That's dead for a reason too," Scott said.

JB, always the one with the vocabulary, said, "Well, how about a masque? Or a revue comedie? An opera bouffe?" He got carried away. "Or a divertissement, a comdie larmoyante, a..."

Len interrupted, "How about a variety?", thus bringing JB back to Earth.

He huffed, "It's pedestrian, but serviceable, I suppose."

The rest of the group agreed.

Then Scott said, "But what do we name our variety show. A variety would be fine if we were in high school, but it would put us at the bottom of the listings in the papers."

"I remember reading a story that Michael Bennett insisted that his show be called *A Chorus Line* so it would get listed in the Times first. That was unless someone came up with a show called the Aardvark someting or other. Why don't we call this the Aardvark Varieties. It gets us first in the trades, and those in the know will get the historical show biz reference."

"Ophelia, you amaze me. I like it," Scott admitted. "So, are we all agreed? It's The Aardvark Varieties. All those in favor? Carried and done."

Trashy put up his hand. "Uh, before we get to carried away, I'd like to know one thing. Can Len sing?" He got off his stool and went to the piano. He played an arpeggio. "Come on over here, Len. Sing for me."

Len got up and went to stand next to Trashy. They quickly decided what to sing as Ophelia and VondaLee went over to join them. Len began to sing.

Scott leaned over the bar and kissed JB on the cheek. "JB, this is a terrific idea. We sure do appreciate it." He slid back. "By the way, I haven't asked. How did it go last night at the porn place?"

"Okay, I guess. That's my graveyard job. I'm their new clerk. I haven't found out a hell of a lot yet. The manager did mention one thing I want to check into. But I need a video camera with a night lens to do it."

"Oh, let me check. I'm sure there's one here behind the bar. Two or three get left every night."

"Thanks, Scott. Sarcasm noted. But I did check the phone book and found a place that has them. I going there from here."

The men applauded as Len hit the last note of his song,

Chapter 13

Len leaned back into the seat and sighed. The cab quickly pulled into traffic and headed for his apartment.

The session with the four queens had lasted for three whole hours. Just listening to them pick and banter and harp and put down each other was exhausting. And, of course, the rehearsal couldn't run smoothly—first there was a hassle with DeDe, who wouldn't let them use the showroom for some unfathomable reason, since the room was empty—her reason was probably just to be a bitch. At least that was the consensus of opinion among the queens. And they would know. Finally she let them in the room, but would only let them light the stage area not the rest of the room. To save electricity she said.

Then there was the problem of the missing piano. That meant they had to find Tom, who had taken the instrument away to build a shelf along the inside of it. Len then had to explain that the addition was part of a bit he planned for the act.

That became cause for a group discussion on the pros and cons of the idea—was it funny? Was it hip? Was it too hip? Everyone had an opinion, with none of them agreeing with the other, which led to more harping, more bitching, and more personal attacks on their persons.

By then it had become perfectly obvious that putting an act together by committee was not going to work. So, deciding that this wasn't a democracy it was show-biz, they concluded—after Len had made it clear that it was his act, his money, and his name at the top of the marquee—that Len would make the final decisions.

Finally after the best part of an hour they could start working. Timing being the essence of good showmanship JB then announced he had an errand of his own to do and he had to leave.

That meant it was left to Len and the queens to piece together a forty-five minute set, plus encores, of their solo bits. With the needed comedy material to fill in between the bits left for JB to write it still took another two hours.

And what they actually had for all their effort was a set of numbers that might work—emphasis on might. That was assuming Len and the troupe could learn the moves, that it all could be tightened and organized, that an actual script could be workrd out, and the queens could stop the incessant bickering with each other long enough to accomplish any part of the above. More rehearsal would prove if once together the act had wings and could fly.

Len watched the city go by his cab window. His mind was now focused on decising what he should do about Cubby's twelve messages he had picked up from his answering service right before he left the rehearsal.

Most actors had switched to machines long ago, but Len believed there was something kind of upper crusty about having a real person responding to a call. That's why he still retained the services of CallMe Answering.

The woman who ran the service also knew everything about Len. His entire sordid story, with all the footnotes, and still she treated him like her long-lost bubbula when he called in. She had said he should respond to Cubby's messages. "So, tell me, darlink, my poopkin, what would it hurt?" she had admonished. But she only wanted to see him with somebody, even Mr. Might-Be-Perfect would do. Len wasn't so sure.

It has been awhile since I've dipped my toe into this sort of relationship folderol, but not without good reason, Len thought to himself. My focus has been primarily on the rebuilding of the career for the last several months, and, of course, that getting sober thing too. That put a mojor crimp in the sex thing, let alone the dating thing.

Then again, it is rather nice to be pursued. Quite unexpected and flattering, especially at this age. When you're twenty it's not questioned. When you're thirty it's accepted. In your late thirties it's nicely unusual. And now? At way too close to forty? Well, it's a relief to know that the hill still needs some climbing before I get over it.

Len leaned forward and gave the driver a new address to drop him off at.

Wait a second, Len continued to himself. Do you really want to get involved in all this? With anyone? It takes huge chunks of time, it asks for tremendous sacrifices, it means making enormous accommodations to someone else's whims and caprices, it's cause for major expenses, and often is a giant pain in the ass. And that was the good parts.

Len leaned forward and gave the driver his apartment address.

Then Len continued thinking. How many more chances are you going to get? Good Lord, fella, you're at the point in gay life where you disappear. There's a point in every gay man's life when he finds himself looked at as if he no longer exists. Other men actually look right through you. You have vanished. You are invisible. You are forty. If you're lucky you might stretch it to forty-five. But there always comes your time.

Len leaned forward and gave the driver another change of address.

But what about the problems? And with Cubby there were certainly problems. Major ones. Drugs. Depression. Can you live with them? Or would there be a possibily of change? Would Cubby be willing? Would I? Does it really matter if he does coke. Hell, most of New York indulges in the stuff. Who am I to be so damned judgemental?

Len leaned forward again with the apartment address.

But what about that attraction to Cubby? And it's strong. Powerful. It takes you over and pulls at you. Tiny fingers urging you toward him. It might be wrong but when was that draw this unrelenting before? It had to be years ago. The sex is just so damn good...

Len leaned forward again.

The driver hit the brakes, hard, for a light. Len was thrown forward and then back in the seat. Okay, I get the point. Len sat back without giving the driver any more directions.

They drove onward, making all the turns needed to get to the Upper East Side. At a point several blocks from his home, Len poked a twenty through the plastic partition and told the cabby to pull over.

A short walk later and he was in front of that familiar hobnailed door. He took a breath, opened it, and entered.

It was still early so the place wasn't full yet. A couple of people sat in one of the banquettes. Empty stools lined the bar. Len took one of the stools slightly further than midway and sat,

The bartender greeted him and took his order. As the drink was placed before him the piano behind him started to play a sweet tinkily tune.

That's when Cubby, giving far more weight to the words than what Mr. Berlin ever could have meant, started to sing...

I Love A Piano, I Love...A...Piano.

Each word, each verse was nauanced and heavy with entandre'—single, double, even triple. Each note was meant only for Len.

I Love To Stop Right Beside An Upright...

Cubby's emphasis gave a sexual meaning to the lines that any censor would never have suspected. Never in a million years would Len have thought of himself as a piano, but he knew he was supposed to.

Or..A High-toned Baby Grand...

Cubby finished his set. He stood up to acknowledge the tepid applause, then stepped from the platform and made a beeline for where Len waited. He stood beside him, leaned in, and whispered into his ear. Len turned to him and instead of a slap, as he had intended in the cab, gave him a kiss. A peck. But not a hostile peck. Minutes later they had seated themselves away from the bar at one of the tables in the back.

"Len, I'm glad you're here," Cubby began, "I was miserable knowing that you were angry with me. We shouldn't do this to each other."

"I wasn't angry so much as I was disappointed. You know my history and exactly why it hurt to watch you doing that stuff."

"What about my history? I won't just roll over and accept that my life is so..so Goddamned dull...not when there's blow around as an alternative."

"But what an alternative."

"Come on, Len, lighten up. For me coke is a way to feel something. It's all in the way its handled."

"And why do you think you can handle it any better than everybody else? I can't tell you how many lives have been destroyed by that stuff. I've seen it. People sit in those AA meeting rooms with their lives in complete shambles because of what coke has done to them. And, believe me, the drug controlled them. And it wouldn't let go until it took everything."

"They let it get to them. They let it control them."

"They're addicts, Cubby. They didn't have a choice."

"Of course they had a choice. Everyone has a choice. Just like you do."

"Coke was never my thing. I didn't snort. My thing was booze. I swallowed."

"So there you are. Drinking was your problem, right? Cocaine isn't booze, so you wouldn't be drinking. If you don't drink then you'll be okay." Cubby leaned in and spoke to Len in a soothing, smoothly hypotic tone. "Len, how much of this disapproval of me is really that program talking?

It isn't your problem it's theirs. Be honest with yourself. You really want to do some of this, but that cult you belong to wouldn't approve."

"Cult? You're calling AA a cult?"

Cubby's answer sounded almost professorial. Like an expert. Dr. Joyce Brothers even. "It meets all the criteria I've ever read on the subject. They have closed meetings. They have special buzzwords and slogans. They look down on anyone outside the group...they call us 'normies', right? There's even a secret code so you know each other. Are you a friend of Bill's? It's the whole schemer, Len. If you don't get with their program...and calling it a 'program' is another indication of it being a cult...just how accepting are they? If you decide to do something they don't approve of would they still call you? Would you still be welcome? Or would they turn on you? Ostracize you? Close ranks against you. It's sounding more and more like a cult, isn't it?"

Len was totally stunned. He ran Cubby's argument up and down a list in his head, comparing what Cubby said to what AA said. Trying to assimilate what Cubby had just proposed. He wondered. Would the group really call if I didn't do what they told me? They say they will, but what about that guy who went out on a slip last week? All they did was nod knowingly and say he'd learn his lesson. Is that reaching out? Of course, they wouldn't do that to me, would they? Or would they?

Cubby reached into his coat pocket and took out a small glass vial. He opened it and tapped a bit of the powder from it onto the space between his thumb and finger. He put it to his nose and took the hit.

Then Cubby tapped another bit onto his

hand and held it toward Len.

Len looked around. Where were the warning sirens? The alarms. Why wasn't the Calvery coming through the door right now? Where were they? There was only quiet. No bells. No whistles. No stop sign. Not even a crossing guard.

Len leaned forward, closed his eyes, and breathed in.

Chapter 14

The Spy Shop, hidden in a back alley on the edge of the Village, had just the item JB needed to install at work that evening. The store clerk, a thin man with a demeanor similar to that of a ferret, took him to a glass case filled with electronic paraphernalia. There were telephoto lenses, cameras, keypads, radios and such.

"What I'm looking for is something that will take pictures in the dark,,,"

"A night or infra-red lens then?"

"If you say so. But it has to be small enough that it won't be noticed. I don't want it stolen."

"I see. Well, let me show you this unit." He reached into the case and brought out an instrument that in size and shape resembled a cigar box with a lens attached to the side. He gave JB a ferral smile and began his pitch. "This micro camera has a built in recorder with a three FPS, 1.5 megapixel SXGA quality CCD camera, a continuous recorder on a 10.2 GB hard drive, and..."

JB felt as if he needed a Berlitz course in electronics, He stopped the salesman. "Excuse me, but I really don't have much expertise in this field. Could you explain that in laymans terms?"

Twenty minutes later JB left the store with the camera. It had cost more than he wanted but suited his needs exactly. The fact it had a matte black enamel finish and was of such a small size made it perfect for the spot he had in mind. The cruising men in the porn store wouldn't even see it.

JB went by foot toward the porn store enjoying both the evening and the neighborhoods ambiance. The streets were filled with people out for their Saturday night revels. It infused the Village with a sense of anticipatiory excitement. There was a festive, almost carnival like atmosphere to wallow in. Add in the strong undercurrent of sexual tension caused by gay men and lesbian women on the prowl and you had an arena that any Roman Gladiator would have felt at home in. Those Roman contests had nothing on New York from Friday night to Sunday afternoon. Let the games begin.

Randy young studs wandered singlely and in packs from bar to bar searching for their soulmates, at least for tonight. Passing by the bars the muffled bass of their sound systems playing the latest mix caused the very air to vibrate.

The restaurants were full inside and out. This was where couples gathered. Sitting two-by-two at tables along the sidewalk, wooden planters of boxwood seperating them from the pedestrians. Sets of men and women sat looking into each others faces, each hoping that the one across from them would stay. That this wasn't their next ex-lover.

Down at the corner a man stood with a box at his feet with a few coins he had managed to beg or scrounge so far. He was singing an enthusiastic, but off-key, operatic aria. His voice wavered and strained to reach each note, but there was about his effort a poignant beauty. His earnestness gave him a modicum of dignity despite his shabby appearance and rum soaked singing. In New York even the unfortunate had talent. Not every talented person who sought his dreams in the city could be a star. Many didn't make it at all. JB dropped the change from his pocket into the man's box and moved on.

What JB couldn't fathom was why none of the searching men that filled the Village that night acted even a little anxious about a madman who was stalking their streets. A man ready not only to capture them, but also to maim and disfigure their bodies before he killed them, and as a final indignity, to paint their corpse a bilious and demeaning lilac. This deranged killer could easily pick any one of them to be that night's victim. But no one seemed worried. They all seemed to have other priorities. These men were out for the night, looking, with various degrees of desperation, for someone. Any someone. Even a someone who might kill them.

The streets got quieter and darker as JB got closer to the porn shop. It was as if the business itself dictated the mood of the surrounding blocks. This was a cruising zone. No parking or laughing in the white spaces.

JB went up the steps to the entrance. Inside the store there was only a heavy silence. No background music or Muzak to dull the senses. The only sound was a distant sporadic moan from the porn movie soundtrack in the theater. The air was heavy with the odor of male pheromones.

Men, each standing alone, stood at the racks and flipped through open magazines or looked over videos. None of them really saw what they looked at. These men had shut down any normal brain activity at the door. Another organ, located lower on their bodies, was now telling them what to do. These men were acting on automatic. None of them spoke or looked at each other, but not one of them missed any single movement made by any of the others.

Then one of them broke from the herd and headed for the desk. He paid his fee and went through the turnstile to the back. Emboldened, two other men did the same, one after the other. The three who had gone inside were soon replaced by three more arrivals. These men were also robots, waiting for thier dicks to tell them what to do next.

JB went to the desk, greeted Brian, and was buzzed onto the deck area where he put his backpack and shopping bag down.

"What's in the bag?," Brian asked.

"This? Just some light bulbs. When I left this moring I noticed that a bunch in the back were burned out."

"Probably just unscrewed. The customers do it all the time. Light disturbs their orgies. But thanks for thinking about it. I'll reimburse you for what you spent."

"Is there a ladder? I can replace the things before you go so I won't have to leave the deck."

Brian gave JB the key to the storage closet, then buzzed him through the turnstile so he could do his chore.

Inside the closet, along with toilet supplies and cleaning gear, JB also found the main lightboard. Locating the right switch he flipped on the one for the back area of the building. Taking the ladder with him he went through the hallway to the back. He wasn't surprised to find the now lit space completely abandoned and everyone crowded into the booths or the theater. That was a good thing, since it meant he wouldn't be bothered while he placed the camera.

Just as Brian had said, the wires from the previous video camera were still hanging from the ceiling. JB only hoped they were still live and would work with his unit. Placing the ladder he carefully climbed up and twisted one of the old cords and his camera's cord together. Nothing. Twisting the second two cords together caused the little red light on the front of his camera to go on. JB breathed a sigh of relief. Then he unattatched the second cords so he could work without getting electrocuted.

JB used the screws provided with the camera and attached the black box to the ceiling. He aimed the lens, re-attached the cords, and checked the viewfinder to make sure he had the back door square in the lens. He also took a piece of electricians tape and covered the little light on the front.

Finished he went back to the main board and turned off the switch. He went back to the area and was pleased to find that the unlit near dark back there made the camera virtually impossible to see. He took the ladder back to the storage room and then went to the front.

Chapter 15

It wasn't only the backdoor alarm going off at four thirty AM in the morning that made JB call the police. It was the other two things also.

First was the object he found when he went to turn off the siren at the back door. Second was what a customer found and brought up to the desk a little bit later. The three incidents put together were what set off alarms in JB's head.

The hour or so it took for the police to get to the store was actually helpful in that it gave JB time enough to again get out the ladder, go to the back and take down the camera he'd placed so he could put it back into it's box. He would have to view the pictures it had taken later. That hour of waiting was also time enough for the news of the imminent arrival of the police to get passed around and to empty the store of customers,

When the police did arrive JB was pleased to see that Detective Peters, the hunk of a cop—and the one he liked—was among them. It should make for, if not a nicer interrogation, then a prettier one.

Peters sipped from a cup of deli coffee. "I'd just started my shift...I didn.t even get my first cup of precinct coffee...and I heard your name on this call. What the hell are you doing in a porn shop?"

"You start work early, don't you Detective?" Peters nodded. "Well, if you must know, I work here. I do the graveyard shift."

Peters looked around the store. "As empty as this place is it can't be much of a job, but I don't think I want to know anymore. That way I don't have to explain anything to the Captain."

"Good idea. He warned me not to get involved in this. If he should ask just say I needed Christmas money."

"In the summer?" Peters, now deciding to get officious, pulled out his notebook. "Okay, Mr. Bent, do you want to tell me why you called this morning? I still have to make a report."

JB explained. "...so when the door alarm went off I had to go back and shut it off. That's when I found this shoe." He sat a brown loafer on the counter. "It was lying back there just outside the door. I thought it was sort of odd. I mean if someone left by that door he would have to be pretty bad off to leave his shoe behind. And it didn't look like some old shoe that someone had thrown away. Not only is it clean, but it's almost new. Well, that got me wondering, let me tell you. Then, about fifteen minutes later, one of the customers brought up this." JB put the second object on the counter next to the shoe. "It's a backpack. The customer found it in one of the booths. Just left there. And it isn"t empty. I checked. Why would someone not take his backpack? I wouldn't leave mine behind,"

"So, you think the two items, the shoe and the backpack, are connected?"

"Yes, I do. I think someone...someone who happened to be the owner of this backpack...was taken out of here by force tonight. And the shoe at the door was his too. He lost it in some sort of struggle when he was taken."

"By force?" Peters chuckled. "Come on, Bent. You're being overly dramatic. This is real life, not one of your novels. It was probably some guy too drunk to remember he was carrying his own backpack. And as for the shoe? Is there a pool of water at the backdoor? The same guy probably slipped and lost this then."

JB took a deep breath meant to calm himself. How dare this cop think he was exaggerating. "Detective Peters..." JB took on a tone deliberately steady. More flies with sugar and all that. "Did Captain DeAngelo tell you that the mummified body we found had tokens from this store wrapped in the folds of the plastic around it?"

"He did. So?"

"Did he also tell you that the mummy was strangled with a purple cord?"

"No, he didn't. But so what?"

"Okay. Call me crazy if you want, but that is all pertinent to this. I apoligize if this sounds like a Saturday afternoon serial to you, but I think The Fairy Dust Killer has been using this place as his own private hunting ground for his victims. He takes them from here, by force if he has to, and carries them off to their doom."

"Pretty melodramitic, don't you think? When does the Masked Marvel come to the rescue?"

"Think what you want." JB reached into the backpack and pulled out a datebook. He flipped a couple of pages. "But, I'll lay you odds that the next Fairy Dust victim will be a young man by the name of Keith McDonnal. And he'll be found soon...maybe even later today. Unfortunately, he's going to miss his brunch date."

"That's total supposition, Bent. What reason can you have for jumping to such a conclusion?"

"Detective, can you think of a better place to find the sort of victims The Fairy Dust Killer prefers than right here? In that backroom? He's got a wide open field of young men willing...in fact, practially begging to let themselves be victimized and captured. And they wouldn't even know what hit them when it happened. It's like a tea cup full of fish for the killer."

"That's your novelist imagination working overtime, Bent."

"Is it? We'll see later this morning, won't we, Detective?"

"Maybe. Right now I have to confiscate these items. If the owner...I mean, when the owner comes back for them tell him where he can pick them up." Peters took the shoe and the backpack and started to leave.

"Detective, I also think the killer takes his victims somewhere close to here. That way he isn't seen with his victim struggling and fighting against him. I hope you'll check around..."

"I'll have my men be on the lookout." Peters turned and left the store. That left JB with his guesses and theories and little else. JB had no choice but to continue his shift until his relief came in later that morning.

JB slammed the cassette into his VCR and waited while it rewound the mornings set of pictures from the porn store exit door. The camera took three single pictures each second. The VCR would then show the images in a fast moving slideshow.

When the single pictures were shown one after the other the TV screen seemed jerky and almost in slow motion, as if you were viewing an old-fashioned nickelodeon movie—*Fatima and the Seven Vails* or How The Fairy Dust Killer Did His Dirty Business.

The pictures flashed on JB's television screen, the infrared lens and the red exit sign giving them all a pinkish glow. It was as if the camera had been set in Hell to capture the torment of the inmates. The exit of the porn store was centered in the frame while shadows of men cruising moved across the lower part of the pictures. At the left of the screen was a time and date indicator in a garish led green color.

At one-forty-one two men used the door as a place to have a sexual encounter. By one-forty-eight they had moved on. Long term assignations were not for the Gayity. There were too many men on display and the next one might be the right one, whatever might constitute right at that particular moment. At two-ten a small group orgy got started and then moved out of camera range and into the darkness,

The pictures continued. Men were touched, judged, rejected, and passed by on the way to another in mili-seconds. At three two men seemed to like what each had to offer. They quickly began a courtship that went on for a fast minute or two.

At first they made out and touched as if they were romantics, their meeting filled with tenderness, then with lust, and finally release. They too then moved on and the screen was empty

JB sped the pictures forward to the time of the alarm going off.

The timer showed four-twenty-three AM when two men—one slightly taller and dressed in black leather, with the other in a tank top and pale chinos—headed for the door. The man in black leather had his arm thrown across his partner's shoulder in what could have been a possesive but affectionate gesture.

The boy in chinos might have been walking willingly with his leatherman. But as they neared the door chinoboy pulled back, seemingly not wanting to go any further. That's when leatherman tightened his hold on him.

Leatherman's arm went quickly around chinoboy's neck and over his mouth to keep him from shouting. Then leatherman leaned sideways so that chinoboy's feet were lifted up and off the floor. Leatherman then pulled chinoboy toward the door. But chinoboy had begun to struggle, pulling at leatherman's arm, trying desperately to work his way loose from the grip holding him captive.

Leatherman turned himself to the right so his body was full against chinoboy's back. He put his other arm over his captives chest and took a step backward, landing his own back flat against the door. Leatherman gripped chinoboy tighter, then used his butt to push on the bar across the door. He slammed it open and stepped backward to get outside.

Chinoboy still fought his captor, his legs bicycling in an effort to get a foothold in the doorway. His flailing and kicking feet caused one of his shoes to drop from his foot. It landed in the doorway and kept the door from closing completely.

The alarm had gone off when the door was pushed and must have been wailing in the background. Then the door was slammed open again by leatherman. He leaned in, looked both ways, kicked chinoboy's shoe out of the way, and pushed against the door to close it. Chinoboy could be seen lying limply in leatherman's arm as the door shut blocking the view of the two of them. This all took place in seconds, the timer hadn't changed to four-twenty-five.

JB rewound the picture and watched again, and then again, his brain shouting at the suddenness of it, then at the utter banality of it. A man's life was gone in less time than it took to catch your breath.

Now JB slowed down the picture by pausing and running the scene a picture at a time. This way he was more able to pick out the details. The chinoboy looked to be about twenty-five, with dark hair, and was good-looking before fear distorted his features. The leatherman's barracks hat covered and shadowed his face, but there was a strong jaw and longish hair pulled back into a tail at the back. What grabbed at JB was something that felt strangely familiar about him. It was in the way he stood and moved. JB sped up the pictures slightly. Then he backed them up and ran them again. Thst's when he was finally able to see what it was that bothered him—the leatherman limped. His right leg was stiff and he dragged it behind him. As each picture rolled by the horror of the situation playing out frame by frame, JB found himself coming to a conclusion he really didn't want to.

When the leatherman turned his body to reach across chinoboy's chest that sense of knowing, but not wanting to know, became even stronger. The unzipped leather coat partly covered the man's body, but couldn't hide his muscled build. Broad shoulders and full arms caused the coat sleeves to shine and ripple in the dim light. Enough of his bare chest was visible to show a deep cleft where the pecs met at the center. The red from the exit light bounced off the six pac of ab muscles that lined his stomach, while a sliver of dark hair cut down the middle and into the belly button.

The final brick fell into place when the leatherman had gone out the door, dragging chinoboy with him. In their struggle chinoboy had knocked leatherman's hat cock-eyed on his head. When he leaned back in to dislodge the shoe stuck in the door he also had looked from first one side to the other. That was when his face was caught fully by the camera. The cap still slightly shadowed the eyes but who the leatherman was became completely unmistakable.

It was Tom.

Chapter 16

Sitting up and rubbing his eyes JB realized that no matter how tired he was sleep just wasn't going to happen. Not when he had to deal with what he knew.

All the tossing and turning he'd done in the last two hours—each toss making him more sure of what he had to do, each turn bringing him closer to the inevitable—hadn't made what he learned about Tom any easier.

How were you supposed to turn in someone you know and like? The old schoolyard rules about being a ratfink keep shouting at you to keep your mouth shut. But grow up. This wasn't elementary school and Tom didn't steal your homework. There actually was no real choice. When someone you know has turned out to be a killer, with , so far, five or maybe six men dead at his hands—what else could you do? You couldn't leave him out there to do it again. How could you live with yourself if you did that?

But, it was crazy. It couldn't be Tom. It didn't seem possible. Tom always appeared to be such a gentle creature. It was as if he'd run away if you raised an eyebrow of disapproval at him. He didn't seem to have the rage in him needed for this kind of killing. And make no mistake, there was major rage going on with the Fairy Dust victims. Had Tom somehow learned to cover that anger? To keep it buried somewhere inside?

It was the pictures that damned him. That video camera didn't lie. It onl;y showed what had actually happened. And it was Tom in that doorway. What was the old saying? If it looked like a duck and walked like a duck, then it had to be Tom. It was Tom who'd left the porn store with that young man lying passed out on his arm.

JB made his decision, He knew that all the doubt and questioning was merely a smokescreen. He knew what had to be done.

He reached for the phone.

A cab ride taken after JB made his phone call had him gingerly climbing the rickety metal stairs at the back of Cherries. He stood in front of Scott's second floor door and knocked.

When he received no immediate answer he knocked again, louder.

Scott, not quite awake and dressed only in boxer shorts, ripped open the door. He groggily mumbled something about why the hell someone was making all this damn noise this frigin' early. And on a dman Sunday too. He shook his head to clear it. "Oh, hello, JB? What's up?"

"I'm sorry to wake you, Scott, but it's important. I have to talk to you about someone.

Someone you know better than I do."

"It must be important. Since we're both working nights you should be asleep the same as me. All right, come on in." He stepped aside and JB went past him to head toward the living room. Scott followed.

Stifling a yawn Scott asked, "Can I get you some coffee? I can re-heat last nights. I could use some."

"Yeah, sure. But first, is Tom here?"

"You mean with me? No, we didn't hook up last night. He was supposed to work the bar but he disappeared..."

JB had an pretty good idea where he had gone too.

"...but I can't do anything about it. He does own the joint. I have no idea if he's in his room."

"So, you haven't seen him...since when? Yesterday evening, right?"

Scott handed over a cup of microwaved black liquid. "That's right. In fact, you saw him around the same time. Right after he sang was when he vanished. What's up?" He took a sip from his cup and made a face. "Good God. Don't drink that JB until I get some milk for it. This stuff tastes like snot on an iceberg."

JB sat the cup down. "Scott, it doesn't matter. I've got something pretty awful to tell you..."

JB explained what he had found out and what he had to do because of it.

Scott's color paled more than usual. "I don't believe it," he said.

"I'm sorry, Scott. But the security camera took pictures. Tom did take a boy from the store."

"You're telling me that Tom. Tom...who can barely hold a job. Who couldn't get by if it wasn't for his sister. Who I've held in my arms like a Teddy Bear...is a killer? Come on, JB."

"That's what I'm saying. And the police are

going to want to talk to him. Did you say he has a room in this building?"

"Yeah. Downstairs. On the next floor."

"Can we check it?"

"Sure, I guess..." Scott looked at his watch. "The outside office door is locked this early. Come on." He took JB to the back of his apartment. Next to the washer and dryer stood a wire cage. Scott pushed a button and the grinding of turning gears was heard starting up.

Pulling a pair of cut-offs from a laundry basket by the washer, Scott slipped into them and said, "We'll take the freight elevator. It stops on the next floor."

"So this elevator runs up and down the entire building?"

"Right. It's a piece of crap that bearly runs, but it does the job." He pulled a T-shirt from the basket where he found the cut-offs and put it on.

The platform arrived at the top floor, Scott and JB stepped onto it. Scott pushed the down button and it shakily made its way to the next floor down. It groaned agonizingly as it stopped.

The space outside the wire cage was dark but Scott soon enough found the switch and turned on a set of overhead lights. The desks that JB and Len had sat at just a few days ago could be seen at the other end of the stacks of bar supplies and beer cartons,

Scott made a turn to the right and headed for the door of the plywood cubical built into the corner. JB then realized what he had first thought was an extra storeroom actually was Tom's home-built bedroom.

Scott knocked. No answer. He called for Tom and got silence.

"I guess he isn't here. Maybe we'd better check the rest of the place. He might be downstairs."

They got on the elevator again and rode it down to the main floor. The back of the bar slid into view. Lez stood in as bartender serving the Sunday morning Bloody Mary and Mimosa people. She obviously heard the elevator as it ground its way down and turned to spot JB and Scott. She waved them off the elevator and came over to them.

Agitated she said, "Will you tell me what's going on around here? In the middle of my early hangover crowd some cop comes in here looking for Tom. It made everyone damn uncomfortable too. Do you know what's up?"

"Lez, it's not good," Scott said. "What did you tell the cop?"

"I told him the truth. That I hadn't seen Tom since yesterday. What do you mean it's not good? Is Tom hurt? Have you seen him?"

"No, but I think I'm grateful I haven't. JB, why don't you take Lez up to the deck and tell her what's going on. I'll take over the bar for now."

Her look was mildly perplexed as she followed JB to the side doorway and up the stairs to the deck used for alfresco drinking. She grabbed a chair off a metal table and sat it down. JB did the same and began to explain what had happened and why the police were looking for her brother,

"No. I won't believe it. No matter what you say. I can't"

"Lez, there's proof. We have pictures of him taking a young man by force,"

"I don't care. You've made a mistake. It isn't Tom."

"It is, Lez. You told me the other day that Tom is all right as long as he takes his medication. Isn't that what you said?"

"So? He takes them. I know he does."

"But what are they for, Lez? You also said that he withdraws when he doesn't take them. What did the doctors say that Tom had? Why does he need the medicine?"

Lez equivocated. "Something is wrong in his head, that's all. But Tom does take the medication. I know he does. In fact, I can prove it."

She got up from her chair and went over to the building. She stepped up to the office door, then reached behind her and took her keyring hanging off a back beltloop of her jeans. She used one of the keys to open the door and gestured JB to follow.

Lez headed directly toward the back area, made a turn and went straight to Tom's cubical. She used another key on her ring and opened his door. She went inside. JB stayed in front, waiting for Lez by her desk.

A few seconds later she came out of the room and walked to where JB was standing. She was staring at her hands. In them she held several amber colored prescription bottles.

JB asked,"Well?"

"This isn't good. There's a couple month's worth of pills here. Tom should have been taking these." Lez sat at her desk and let the bottles fall from her hands. JB picked one of them up.

"This is Chlorpromazine, Lez. The doctors didn't just say that Tom had something wrong in his head. They told you exactly what it was."

She continued to stare straight ahead.

"Scott said that Tom told him he hears a voice. Schizophrenia does that. Is that what it is?"

JB slammed his hand on the desk. Lez started as the sound echoed in the room. "Answer me."

Sounding as if she was pulling something from a deep pocket Lez began to talk. "The doctor's said that it was the accident. The one that killed Timmy...they were lovers, you know? Tom and Timmy...the accident caused the onset of the schizophrenia. But it had been there all along, for years, waiting for something to trigger it. Tom has been in the hospital...at least thirty times. But he's better now. This medicine has been a Godsend. It really helps him stay on an even keel."

"When he takes the medicine, Lez. When he doesn't he's capable of anything. He's at the mercy of that voice he hears. That voice could be telling him anything. Even to kill."

"I don't believe it, JB. Tom is a gentle man. He can't be doing this. He can't be this Fairy Dust Killer. He can't." Her denial had strong ties on her mind. It blinded her to the obvious.

JB moved behind Lez's desk to the wall covered in pictures. He took down the framed photo of Tom and Timmy. He held it out to Lez.

"In this picture the boys are wearing light colored sweaters. The picture is in black and white so I can't tell. What color were their sweaters, Lez?"

She stared at the picture for a moment, then looked up at JB. Her mouth opened but at first there was no sound. She swallowed hard and said, "Oh, God. It was lilac. It was an in-joke. A way of telling everyone they were gay. Tom and Timmy always wore it. It was their color. Oh, my God. Forgive me."

Chapter 17

A passionate pink fingernail poked JB on the shoulder. "Wake up, hon. You've been out here for hours. Since Lez left me behind the bar. What are you doing?"

"Huh? What? Oh." JB crawled up from his deep sleep. "I just meant to close my eyes for a moment. I didn't get any sleep last night." He rubbed at his eyes. "Good God, what the hell are you wearing?"

Scott was standing in front of him in a drag nightmare. Worse than anything even Milton Berle could have come up with in his heyday. A red checked tablecloth was wrapped and knoted at his waist, two honeycomb yellow paper pineapples were stuck to his bare chest, and circles of strung fruit—lemon zests, cherries, orange slices, plus a few green olives with pimentos—hung around his neck. On his head was a bar towel wrapped as a turban with a bunch of grapes and several bananas cascading from it. Two lemon zesters served as earrings. His makeup consisted of huge cupidsbow painted lips, pink doll like circles on each cheek, arched upside down V's for eyebrows, and comic flapping eyelashes.

"Oh, this? When Lez left I couldn't get into drag like I usually do. So the customers had a 'Dress The Queen' contest. I was the queen. The pineapples are from our Hawaii night, the fruit is from the corner deli." He finished with a hand on each hip and a thick Bette Davis drawl, "So, whatta' ya think, huh?"

"Oh, it's stunning...at least I'm completely stunned. But you can give me one of those bananas. I missed breakfast. Did you say Lez left you?"

"Yeah, after you two talked she was pretty upset, so she left, looking for Tom, I guess."

"That's why I stayed here. Tom has to come back here sometime. Then maybe we can talk to him and get him some help."

Scott sat beside JB. "It's still pretty hard to believe."

"I know it is. But with Tom's illness there's no telling what he's capable of."

"Illness? But it was brain damage from his accident, wasn't it?"

No. Lez admitted the doctors have diagnosed Tom as a schizophrenic. That accident was the trigger that caused the onset of the disease."

"The accident caused it, huh? Well, there were all kinds of rumors surrounding that whole thing."

"There were, were there? Jeez. now this is one of the reasons I hang out with Len. This is his area of expertise. He could fill me in...he loves gossip."

"Well, what card carrying queer doesn't. I can tell you most of it. But what about Len? Where is he? There was a rehearsal this afternoon but he hasn't shown up."

"Really? That's not like him. Then I haven't talked to him since yesterday so he could be anywhere. I guess I could call his place."

"Great."

"But only after you fill me in on these rumors you mentioned."

"Simple." Scott leaned in. "Tom and Timmy were not just partners, you know? They were lovers too, and had been together for ages when they had that accident."

"I knew that. Lez told me eariler."

"Oh. Then did she mention that Tom was driving the car? They were on the Pacific Coast Highway out in California. It's a road that's been cut out of the cliffs that face the ocean, with more twists and turns than an orgasmic snake. Well, Tom lost control on one of the turns and rammed the car into a mountainside. Timmy was killed instantly. But the rumor has always been that Tom lost control of the car because Timmy was going down on him while he was driving. They crashed just as Tom got off."

"Where have I heard this before? That story has been around since Cecil B. DeMille filmed his first orgy. It's a Hollywood myth."

Scott posed with a limp wrist. "In thith caseth it isn'th a myth. I'th...I mean I've been to bed with Tom, JB. Believe me, it happened. Or something like it anyway. Tom really does have the top part of his dick missing. When the car hit that mountain Timmy's jaw must have snapped and took off the top of Tom's cock. He still has enough to function, but part of it's gone."

"My God. And so another piece of the puzzle falls into place. That's why the Fairy Dust Killer's victims have all been castrated. He's trying to retrive what's been lost."

"Maybe...it's awfully symbolic, but I do have to admit it fits. Okay, JB, I did my part. Now you call Len and see why he isn't here. All the guys are waiting inside."

"Sure. But I doubt he'll be home or he'd be here. But I'll check." They walked to the stairs and went down to the bar.

Seconds later a dark leather clad figure came around the corner from the back. Clinging hard to the side of the building he headed toward the office door.

Tom's face showed his usual fear, but now there was something else too—a look of disbelief and shock, as if he'd finally realized what he had done. That realization must have required a price he didn't want to pay because panic was clearly guiding his actions. His hands, usually pushing back the hair on his forehead, were now held tightly over his ears, as if he was trying to keep out something too terrible to hear.

Hestumbled on toward the door, then stopped. Sliding down the wall into a crouch he laid his head on his knees becoming a tight ball. He began to rock as a moan came from deep inside him.

"No, I can't. I won't. Don't make me, please." Tom's hands slapped at the sides of his head, still trying to block out what only he could hear being shouted at him. He made a sudden break and ran to the office door. Once there he fumbled in his pocket for the key. A cry, a sound of raw fear,

escaped from him. He beat his fist on the metal shell of the door.

"I am a good boy," he cried. "I've always listened…but not now…I won't. Please. I can't"

He inserted the key into the door, turned the knob and pushed it open. He jumped inside, then grabbed at the door, ready to slam it against the demon's voice. He turned back and leaned out. He held his hands to his mouth and shouted to no one, "Leave me alone."

Then he kicked at the door, swinging it shut on a voice and a threat that only he could hear.

JB stopped on the stairs up to the deck when he spotted the oxfords and grey suit trousers of someone sitting at the table he had vacated to make his call.

Len hadn't been at home, or hadn't answered JB's call, and that was worrying. Len wasn't supposed to do this sort of flaking off of appointment anymore. He had taken a vow of responsibility when he got sober, sort of like a nun's vow of chastity, but without the chaste. He had promised he would be the opposite of his drunken self and show up where he was supposed to be and on time. And he had been doing that more often then not. That's why his not making the rehearsal today was troubling. Now, this set of legs on Cherries deck was the cause for several more questions to pop up.

JB went through the possibilities. Not Lez—the legs were too long. Not Scott—he was still downstairs. It couldn't be Len—he wouldn't be caught dead in a pair of generic brown oxfords. It sure wasn't Tom—he wore black motorcycle boots and dark jeans.

Another step up the stairs revealed the legs belonged to another familiar person.

"Well, hello, Detective Peters." The hunky

policeman sat up straighter—and brought up another one of the lingering questions on JB's mind. Is this handsome detective—with a build like every gayman's late night fantasy—gay or straight? "I didn't expect to find you sitting on a Greenwich Village gay bar deck on a Sunday morning."

"This area used to be my beat, before I went to Homicide. I like to keep up with what's going on in the old neighborhood."

"Humm, you know, it's hard to think of the Village as being a neighborhood. A gaudy, rococo, silver-tinseled, twinkle-lit ghetto maybe."

"Actually, with a job like mine, I tend to see all of New York as one neighborhood after another. Each set of streets has it's own personality. Try to compare the Upper East Side and Delancy Street. It doesn't work. But what I really don't like is this Fairy Dust Killer case. It's caused my old neighborhood to become a fearful place."

"You're right, Detective. But it'll be over pretty soon. As soon as I can find a certain someone and talk with them."

"That explains why you've been hanging out on this deck all morning?"

"Yes. That's right. Wait? All morning?" JB had a questioning look as he crossed his arms over his chest. "Detective Peters, you just got here. How did you know I'd been here that long?"

"I was by here eariler and I saw you. By the way, one of the first lessons they teach in stake-out school is that falling asleep won't help catch the person you're looking for."

"Yeah, I heard that. But I haven't been to bed since I got off work this morning. And working graveyard seems to require more sleep than normal."

"You don't have to worry about that anymore. The porn store was shut down as of ten AM this morning. It turns out you were right about the boy whose backpack you found. He did miss that brunch he was supposed to be at. But you were wrong about him turning up as a vic. There hasn't been a Fairy Dust body found this morning."

"Yet, you mean."

Peters looked at his watch. "It's not morning anymore. It is now officially afternoon. Anyway the store was closed because the boy went missing from there and there might be some evidence left behind. The crime scene boys are there now. So, on the one hand, you'll be able to get a whole lot of aleep now. But on the other hand, you won't be saving that Christmas money you needed."

"There is evidence, Detective. But I have it at my place...on a VCR cassette. I set up a video camera in the store last night."

"You did? That was pretty smart of you. Maybe you're not just a pretty face."

JB looked at Peters, mildly surprised. Was he aware of what he'd just said? Or was it just a joke? He had to realize the implications of it. I mean the man is gorgeous, not an idiot. And he used to work around the Village, so he has to know what he could be intimating. Is he actually flirting? Now this is getting interesting.

The detective broke into JB's thoughts. "What does the camera have to show, Mr. Bent?"

"Well, Detective, it...listen do we have to be so formal? I'm JB. Call me that, please. And do I have to keep calling you Detective? What's your first name?"

"I don't like it but it's Needham. An old

family name passed down and I got stuck with it. If it was shortened it always made me sound like a charity case...Needy. And the other alternative was Ham...considering my profession the fewer pork references the better. So I don't use my first name at all."

"Oh, well, then I'll have to come up with something els..."

"What the hell?" Detective Peters was up and heading across the deck. He stepped over the boxwood hedge that seperated the deck from the sidewalk like a college hurdles runner. He then headed down the street toward the front of the bar where a crowd could be seen gathering. JB followed right behind to check it out with the detective.

A crowd of ten or so people were milling in front of Cherries. A couple were looking up and pointing. Another of them, a greasy looking fat man, shouted, "Yeah, baby, that's it, do a dance. Come on, sexy."

JB looked up. His eyes went wide. Shock made him capable of only one thought. Oh my God, this is the last thing I wanted to happen.

Standing barefoot, on the thin edge of the roof surrounding the top of the building, and maintaining, at best, a precarious and wobbly balance, was Tom.

Chapter 18

Lez's cry could be heard from behind the crowd of people surrounding the front of Cherries. "Tommeee..." Then she started to push people aside so she could make her way to the front of the swelling crowd.

A few paces behind her, like a Mandarin's mistress, DeDe followed.

"Oh, great," JB said, "That's Tom's sister. She'll be a total nutbag about this. Tom's welfare is her main occupation."

Detective Peters turned to him. "You'll have to take care of her, JB. Me...I'm going to go up there on the roof. Maybe I can talk him down." Peters held up his walkie-talkie. "I've called the rescue squad. They'll be here pretty soon. Now, how do I get up there?"

There were loud shouts from the crowd as Tom ripped off his T-shirt and threw it down to the mob. A voice behind JB said, "Jeez, what a body that guy's got. What a stud."

JB answered the detective. "I guess the only way up there is from the stairs on the deck. Please try. Tom is the person I've been waiting for. It's important we get to talk to him. You go on, I'll do my best to keep Lez under control."

Peters nodded. Then he ran and disappeared over the hedge to the deck.

A few seconds later Lez, having finally pushed through the crowd, grabbed onto JB's arm. He turned and put his own arms around her. She stood, staring at the rooftop in silence. Her eyes were wide with fright. DeDe stood behind the two of them grimly staring up. At Tom's next movement she pointed, "What's he up to now?"

Tom had pulled open the buttons on his jeans, shoved them down and stepped out of them. The crowd below applauded wildly. He swung the pants around his head like a lasso, then threw them away. They floated down toward the crowd. It roared it's approval. Now, wearing only white briefs, Tom bent to pick up something from the roof. When he had it in his hands he rose up to stand with his arms raised high over his head. In them was an open unlabeled gallon sized tin can.

The crowd below, not sure what was happening, egged him on. "Yeah, sexy," they yelled. "What's in the can?...What is it, honey?...I'll take some of that. Go for it, stud...."

Lez, near hysteria, turned on the crowd screaming, "What are you people, crazy? You're jackals. Can't you see he's in danger? He's going to fall."

A voice responded, "Aw, come on, honey, lighten up. It's a stunt. This is all for us. Maybe he'll show his ass next."

DeDe, disapproval coloring her tone, shook her head. "They think this is some sort of show. They'll be surprised." She pointed up to Tom. "Look."

Tom now tipped the silver can he was holding. Out of it poured a heavy colored liquid—a particular shade of lilac paint.

The ghastly Fairy Dust paint spilled onto his head, then his shoulders, and down over the rest of his body. The paint spread over his chest. It covered his stomach. The bilious color made him look as if he might be some perverse cartoon character. A muscular pale lavender avenger. The paint continued to pour over his body to his thighs and feet, and finally over the edge of the building, leaving a web of lavender streams against the red of the brick siding.

The crowd, expecting something else from his show, turned on him and shouted their disappointment. "What the hell is that?...That's totally gross, man...What's up with you?"

As for Tom, his attention had been drawn elsewhere. He turned his back on the crowd. Then he started to move away from where he was standing. He backed away like a tightrope walker, moving away from something he saw on the roof. That's when Detective Peters could be seen approching, getting closer to Tom's retreating figure.

On the ground Lez turned to JB. "Who is that? He's frightening Tom."

"It's the police. He's trying to help."

"But he's scaring him, JB. Tom's balance isn't very good since the accident. And with that sticky paint all over him. Please, JB, he's gong to fall. He'll be hurt."

"What can I do?"

DeDe, who had been watching Tom do his balancing act with an expression that bordered on the expectation of disaster, offered her own suggestion. "Maybe you should go up there, JB.

Your a man. It's your job isn't it? To be all brave and stuff. Anyway, he knows you. You wouldn't scare him."

Lez leaped on the idea. "Yes, JB, you go. Tom won't be scared of you. He'll listen to you."

Giving DeDe a thank you but your suggestion is about as welcome as a fart at a christening look, JB said, "Uh, Lez, I'd like too, but I'm really not very good with heights. They make me..."

Lez implored. "JB, you have to. Please. He'll get hurt if you don't. Please..." DeDe smiled, the evil dripping from her lips. JB contemplated a sharp kick to her nether region. "Please," Lez begged him, with a perfectly timed tear streaking her cheek.

JB reluctantly nodded. He let go of Lez, turned, and walked down the block to the boxwood hedge fronting the deck. He looked back, hoping for a reprieve, but saw only the hopeful expression on Lez's face. And a self-satisfied smirk on DeDe's.

Resigned, or rather stuck, JB stepped over the hedge. Crossing the wooden deck to the stairs he looked up to find out where Tom was now standing. He had continued moving backward and had now reached the corner of the roof. This was actually safer for him since it provided him with better footing on the two edges.

JB also saw Detective Peters a few feet away from Tom. He was standing but crouched and talking in the soothing tones one usually would reserve for small children and old ladies. "Now come on, Tom, you don't want to do this..."

Frantic, Tom shouted back at him. "You don't get it, Mr. Man. They're after me. All of them. They want to destroy me. I've got to get away."

"Who are they, Tom? Who's after you?"

Tom pointed at him and yelled, "You're one of them. You know you are. You want to hurt me. I've been told. I know who you are."

"Tom, you're wrong. I won't do anything to hurt you. I'm a friend. I just want to help."

Peters tried taking a step toward Tom. He backed off when Tom's agitated reaction to his move got him to move further along the narrow ledge. He moved too quickly. It caused Tom to lose his balance. He wobbled and swayed a foot out over the empty space of what was a two-story fall onto the hard concrete below.

The crowd on the street caught it's collective breath. Then like a circus acrobat Tom regained his equilibrium, put both feet back on the edge of the roof, and stopped swaying. There was a cry in his voice as he said, "You can't help me, man. You're no friend. That's what the leader told me. No one is my friend. No one can help me. I'm alone in this. I have to get away. I have to."

Below them, JB put his foot on the metal stairs and suddenly remembered, in a blinding flash of anxiety, how rickety and unstable these stairs felt the last time he used them. When was that? Oh, yeah, only a few hours ago."

He took a couple of steps up but stopped when he clearly heard metal creak. I'm not so sure that this is a good idea, he was thinking. It's not like I'm some Sumo wrestler. I'm no heavyweight. Creaking shouldn't be happening. I'm only a pound or two more than I should be, for crip's sake.

He took a few more steps and got more squeals from the stairs in return.

Okay, maybe it's more like ten pounds.

More steps got him more metal scraping sounds.

All right, already, but it's no more than fifteen pounds, max. You've got to give me that. I promise I'll go to the gym tomorrow. I'll lift weights until I melt if I have to.

He swiped his now generously sweaty palms on his pants. He left two streaks of rust picked up from the rails of the stairs. There was no more thinking, this is not good.

The stairs groaned another scraping noise. JB shuttered. He had now realized these stairs were attached to the side of the building by only a couple of rusty bolts. And even worse, he could see those very bolts were able to shift around in their holes. This shifting caused bits of brick dust to fall and float about in the air.

Okay, I think a small degree of panic might be appropriate here. A fluttery feeling ran around his body.

JB forced himself to contiue to the top of the stairs. Once there he leaned against the solid feel of Scott's door. It gave his stomach a chance to fall back to it's accustomed place. Then he realized what he had to do next. His heart dropped down to join his stomach.

He was expected to climb up onto the thin little railing that edged this stairway from Hell, and step out over two stories of empty air to another not very stable looking metal ladder that was attached directly to the side of the building. This latest torture device led up to the roof.

They have got to be joking!, his mind yelled. Let's look at some other options! Going back down might be an idea. JB looked back. No, that would mean I'd have to use those damn stairs again. I could jump? Naw, that wouldn't kill me, it would only maim me for life. So, there's really only one way.

JB took a breath, climbed up on the railing, and feeling like a cowardly Tarzan hanging onto a slippery vine, grabbed hold of the ladder. He swung out, and clung to a rung desperately. Then, one rung at a time, he climbed to within reach of the top edge of the building.

During JB's climb from the deck the detective and Tom had continued playing their dangerous game. The detective would take a step forward—Tom would move away from him. The detective would step back—Tom would stay where he was. But these moves had brought Tom further along the roof edge so that he was over the deck side of the building, closer to where JB was clinging to the ladder.

From his perch JB could hear the detective cajoling Tom. "All right, Tom, I believe you. You've heard a voice. And it's telling you to do this. But, the voice lies, Tom. It's a voice that only you can hear. It's just in your head. Don't listen to it."

"But it's the leader, Mr. Man, yes it is. I have to listen. The voice controls it all. You. Me. Everything."

"No Tom, listen to me. We can get you help. Come with me. Please."

"No, Mr. Man. You want to hide me away in a ward. I've done that. It doesn't help. I won't go. No, sir. I don't need to. I just have to do what the leader tells me. The leader is my guide."

A block away the whine from a rescue truck siren came closer. Tom heard it and turned from the detective to look toward the sound. JB, within inches of where Tom was standing, reached up and grabbed at Tom's ankle. He brushed his leg but failed to grab hold.

Tom, startled, first looked down at JB, and then back up as Detective Peters, seeing an opening, leapt forward.

Tom, sensing the man coming at him, pulled away with a quick motion. That jerk caused Tom to lose his balance again. His arms flailed and his feet flew out from under him. He fell. Backward. Off the edge of the building.

His fall was broken when Tom crashed onto the stair balcony in front of Scott's door. He remained still for a moment, then sat up and shook his head to clear it.

JB shouted at him, "Tom, are you all..."

The stairs, having absorbed the weight of Tom's fall, began to groan and tremble under him. Then came the popping sound of the tired bolts that held the stairs to the building finally giving way. The stairs, no longer held to the bricks, started to lean outward. At first by inches, then by feet. The gap between the building and the staircase widened.

JB, ignoring his fear, climbed down his ladder and reached out. His hand was only a foot away from Tom. "Tom, grab hold."

Tom made a move to reach toward JB. His shifting weight caused the stairs to screech and seperate further away from its already precarious mooring. Tom, now on his knees, reached toward JB. There was a space of about five inches between Tom's hand and JB's. JB stepped down another rung and reached again.

JB heard the final squeal from the staircase. Tom moved further and further from JB's reaching hand.

For what seemed like forever there was only silence. Then, deafeningly, came the sound of metal rubbing, screeching, crashing against itself. The stairs collapsed and fell. Tom went with them, down to the wooden deck below. Then the silence returned.

As the dust from the crash began to settle JB could see Tom lying in the rubble below. He was on his back, covered in the lavender paint he had poured over himself. He looked like a dusty purple splotch with a pointed piece of the stair railing sticking from his chest. Dead.

The silence was broken when Lez, coming around the corner and onto the deck, began to scream. It was an agonized sound that went on as if it would never stop.

Chapter 19

The taxi stopped in front of JB's apartment. He was home. Blessed home. Somehow he gathered what strength he had left and crawled from the cab. He felt beyond tired, what with all that had happened since leaving the porn store—was it only that morning? Right that moment his only focus was getting into his apartment and lying down for at least the next week. Lifting each iron heavy foot required a Herculean effort from him.

As he approched the front door he stopped. A chill was crawling up his spine. He felt as if he had just stepped out of H.G. Wells' time machine. He was back several years before and had just returned home after another fruitless search for his then lover. This unsettling and unwelcome sense of deja-vu was upon JB because of what he'd found in the potted bush beside the door.

Slung into the plant was a sports jacket. Maybe it was an ordinary old sports jacket—no big deal—except it had these badly wrinkled sleeves caised by their being pushed up the wearer's forearms in that casual look JB had seen countless times before. He picked up the coat and looked at the label. He recognized the name. It was one of Len's favorite designers. JB didn't like one bit what this might mean.

He pulled out his keys to unlock the door, then saw he wouldn't need them after all. There was an abandoned set of keys already hanging from the lock. A sigh echoed inside his head as he pushed open the door.

JB had indeed stepped back to the past. Just like he had done times beyond number he found Len crumpled in a heap, reeking of alcohol, passed out on the tile floor in front of the stairs.

"You mother-frigging son of a bitch." JB could feel all the anger he had managed to squash when Len got sober come out from its hiding place and do it's happy dance.

JB was sorely temped to leave Len right where he was. Maybe he'd be tripped over and kicked by the other tenents in the building. Maybe he'd be peed on by a dog being taken for his walkies. It's what Len deserved the cum-sucking, dip-wad-grabbing, sodomistic, ass-kicking, piss, shithole, fucking...

Instead JB found his door key, went down the hall to his own door, unlocked it, and opened it. Then he went back to where Len lay, bent over his prostrate body, lifted him as if he were a sack of vegetables, and carried him inside.

He carried Len through the bedroom and into the bathroom, where he flung him down into the tub. Len didn't even wake. He barely stirred.

JB looked down at him and shook his head. Then he reached over and turned on the cold water shower faucet to full force. That accomplished he went out to the kitchen to make coffee. Coffee for the both of them.

Two cups of expresso strength coffee later

JB returned to the bedroom and sat on the bed. He looked over at the bathroom doorway.

First he heard a moan, then coughing—the beast lives—then JB heard a bit of thrashing, some cursing, and the water being turned off.

Seconds later Len stood in the doorway, soaked to the skin, his sweater-vest stretched down to his knees, his hair flat to his head, and a drip of water running off the end of his nose.

"Was that absolutely necessary?," he said.

JB looked at him as he laid back on the bed. "You're making puddles all over the carpet."

Len made a sweeping bow and backed up into the bathroom. "Forgive me, your worship, but I seem to have fallen into a frigging moat... you son of a bitch." He leaned against the door jam and moaned, "God, I had forgotten how awful this feels. Death, come for me..."

"Cut it out, Len. There's coffee on the bureau there. It'll help. But, I'll tell you right now, you'll get no sympathy from me. No more. Len, how could you? Months of soberity gone. Down the tubes. What on Earth made you destroy that?"

"If you'll put away that superior attitude you've got going there I'll tell you what happened."

"First, get out of those wet clothes. There's a robe hanging on the door."

Len stepped back into the bathroom and emerged a few minutes later wrapped in JB's robe and holding the cup of coffee to his lips.

"God, who taught you to make coffee? Lucrezia Borgia?"

"Shut up and drink it. It's medicinal. Now explain."

"If you want to know the plain and simple

truth...I was thirsty."

"Right. I guess that makes as much sense as any other reason. At least in Len world."

"JB, it is that simple. I wanted a drink. That was it. So I had one. But that wasn't enough...it couldn't be enough, could it? So I had another, and another...and then I lost count. Then I lost the entire evening. I have no idea where I went or what I did last night."

"Sounds like an addiction to me."

"You know, all the way up until that very moment, when that first drink hit my gullet, there was a little part of me that didn't really believe I could be a falling down in the gutter drunk." Len sat beside JB. "Well, that's over. Cubby handed me that coke, and..."

"Wait a minute. Cubby handed you a Coke? How was that a problem?"

"Cocaine, JB. Not cola."

"Oh. Then you both went missing?"

"No. Cubby was at the club and...what do you mean, missing?"

"What night was last night?"

"Huh?"

"Len, was it or was it not a Saturday? First the matinee, and then..."

Len paled. "Oh no. I missed the Greenhouse performance..."

JB nodded. "I would guess the producers, and I might add the Equity rep for the show, aren't very happy with you this morning. About the only person who I can think of that might be happy is your understudy."

"I'm sure. That bitch."

"I'll bet you he did an excellent job too. Len, if you didn't show up for curtain and didn't even call in, I can guarantee you've been reported to

Equity. They will probably file charges against you tomorrow."

Len moaned.

"You only have yourself to blame, honey. You can't even blame Cubby for this one."

Len shook his head. "I know you're right. But that's only the tip of this iceberg. I also have finally figured out that Cubby is bad for me. Really bad. The same as cats."

"I have no idea what the hell you're getting at."

"He's like an allergy, JB. I love cats, but I can't be around them. I can't even sit through a performance of the show *Cats*. My eyes swell and I can't breathe. Well, Cubby's like that for me. Just the same."

"It must be really interesting inside your head, Len."

"But, how do I get rid of the cat, JB?"

"You'll come up with something I'm sure. Maybe you'll find it a good home somewhere?"

Len looked thoughful. "But, maybe it doesn't want a home."

JB reached over to punch Len on the shoulder. "What you really need to do is figure out some excuse that will satisfy Equity. Or you could bite the bullet and pay the fine their going to impose."

"The fine. Ow. Well, maybe I can make enough from the caberet act to cover it."

"That's another thing you missed. You were supposed to have a rehearsal with the group."

"Did I? Oh, hell. I did, didn't I? Boy, I'll bet Scott and the boys are too pissed at me to work with me anymore."

"That's not it. I think they'll be okay. There was enough going on at the bar today that they weren't put out that badly. But, sweetheart, I'm not so sure the whole cabaret thing is going to happen at all."

"What does that mean?"

JB then explained what all had happened at Cherries that day.

"You've got to be joking, JB. That lovely young man has turned out to be the killer? I don't believe it."

"That's was, Len. He's dead. From the fall."

"Oh, no. That's so sad."

"And Lez...and Scott too...would certainl;y agree with your disbelief. Hell, even I find it hard to figure. But there are pictures of him grabbing that boy and taking him from the porn store."

"But, that doesn't necessarily mean that he killed him, does it? Where is this boy? Has his body been found?"

"You know, you're right. That boy hasn't turned up. Where could he be?"

"Could be anywhere."

"And there's something else that isn't right."

"What, for instance?"

"For instance, that missing boy is the wrong type. Tom had a thing for blonds. From his first singing partner and first lover on to his last. Scott. Who is also blond and pale. The boy that was taken was dark. In fact, all The Fairy Dust Killer's victims have been dark. A person doesn't change his preference."

"That's true. Like you and your redheads. Me? I don't really have a type."

"You do. They have to be breathing. You know what else isn't right about Tom and the killer?"

Len shook his head.

"The tongues. The Fairy Dust Killer cuts out the victims tongues. That doesn't make any sense with Tom. What does it signify? Unless it could be the singing...but why? Tom sang, so it wouldn't be a case of looking for something he'd lost, like the killers ritual castration of the victims."

Len yawned. "JB, I'm exhausted. Can we deal with this after we get some sleep? You look like you could use some yourself."

"I don't know. This coffee has got the wheels turning. I'm not sure I can go to sleep." But he put the cup on the nightstand and slid down under the covers anyway. He pushed at his feather pillow getting it shaped just right for his head.

Len stood up, went to the other side of the bed, took off his robe, and slipped under the covers himself. "Well, I'm going to try to sleep. You should too."

JB laid his head into the depression he had formed on his pillow. "Okay, I'll try. But don't count on..."

Before Len had plumped his own pillow and settled into position he heard JB snoring.

Chapter 20

There was a noise intruding on JB's sleep. He reached out to turn off the alarm, then shifted his direction when he realized it was the phone that was waking him. He picked it up, turned over onto his back, and mumbled a nearly coherent, "Hello?"

The voice on the other end brought him out of his fog. "Yes, Lez, I'm awake. Are you all right?"

She replied, "I'm okay, but I'm calling to ask you for help. The police called this morning...A Captain DeAngelo...and he needs me to go to the station and identify Tom. Since you were there yesterday with the other policeman, I thought you might help me. DeDe said she wouldn't go. I can't do this by myself. Could you, JB?"

He looked over at the clock—it was only seven-thirty AM. He rubbed at his eyes. "Uh, I guess..." Then, curiosity finally outweighing his desire to return to sleep, he said, "Yeah, sure, Lez. I'll help. When do you have to be there?"

"They said anytime between now and noon. Is that all right? JB, I hate this. Do I have to do it?"

"I think you do, Lez. Especially if you

want to have Tom taken over by a private funeral home."

JB heard her catch her breath. She continued with a barely suppressed sob. "Okay. Can we meet there? In about an hour. I want to get this over with."

"That should give me enough time. I'll see you then. Goodbye."

"Are you making dates with strange men this early, JB?"

He turned to face Len who was still lying next to him. "Oh, Sorry to wake you, Len. No that was Lez. From Cherries. She wants me to help her with the police this morning."

"Whatever for? Why doesn't that dislikeable wench of a partner she lives with go with her?"

"I don't know. She said DeDe wouldn't go, that's all. It isn't very supportive of her, is it?"

"It's always during the crunch times that you find out how people really feel. Even lovers."

"Maybe DeDe has a fear of dead people."

"Or the police. Or of being a nice caring person. Or of being there when you're needed."

"Whatever. It's between Lez and DeDe, not me. I have to get dressed." JB went to his closet. "What are you doing today?"

"Well, for one thing I have to go to an AA meeting. It's not a happy thought, and it's damned embarrassing, but I'll have to start counting days again."

JB looked over at his friend. "Hallelujah."

"I meant what I said, JB. I think I've got it now. It's finally sunk in. I'm a drunk...a falling down, passing out, not very attractive, drunk... and any magic that booze may have held lost all the glitter it still had over this week-end. I can see the alcoholic underbelly, and it's the color of ugly. Besides, I like what I get from being sober. I almost lost all that last night."

"Maybe it'll be easier for you now, Len. You won't be looking for something that isn't there."

"I hope so." He slapped his forehead. "Oh, hell. I've still got to do something about that Equity charge too."

"Such as?"

"Don't be surprised if the evening papers announce that I've been hospitalized overnight for something debilitating but not lethal."

"Not very honest of you."

"Which would you rather see? A nice little filler about me being sick and unable to perform...which Equity will accept as a defense for their charges...or a three inch headline on Page Six that shouts I have succumbed once again to temptation and have drugged and boozed myself into oblivion and out of show business?"

"I get you. You'll just have hope that you can bribe your doctor."

"JB, he's a showbiz doctor. Of course he can be bribed. Probably for the price of a couple of tickets to the show."

"Then you'll get off easy...this time."

"And I have absolutely no plan's for needing another time, thank you very much."

JB headed for the bathroom. "From your mouth to Jehovah's hope chest."

As they walked down the hall JB put his arm around the shoulders of a very distraught Lez. It was obvious it had been difficult for her to see Tom in his current condition. Most morgue

attendants are not known for neatness and tiny stitches while closing and sewing up a cadaver after an autopsy.

Lez's face was pallid with grief. The grip with which she held the plastic baggy of Tom's few possessions had caused her knuckles to turn white. The bag held only a few objects since Tom died wearing only briefs, but Lez carried the baggy as if it had great weight.

When they neared the door to the outside they passed a group of five or six cops. Some were in uniform, some were not. One of the nots was Detective Peters.

The group was standing around the police headquarters equivalent of the office water cooler—a ten gallon coffeepot. A round of laughter erupted as JB attempted to catch the detectives eye, hoping he would come over to them. But Peters studiously avoided making eye contact. Humm, JB was thinking, what's up with that?

That was when one of the group—obviousily the loudest mouth of the group—made a crude remark for all of them to hear. It meandered along the line that what an interesting couple JB and Lez made. One of the other cops added that he wasn't sure which of the two was the man.

Then Peters added, for some unfathomable reason, "They'll have to flip a coin to decide which one wears the bridal gown." This was cause for another outbreak of laughter.

JB took in the group while his eyes narrowd and a tough smile appeared. He guided Lez over to a bench, put his bag down next to her, and asked her to wait a moment. He then walked up to Peters and tapped him on the shoulder.

Peters turned with a smile, which changed to a startled expression when he saw it was JB.

"Actually Detective..." JB said to him, "... under these circumstances, ones that you are well aware of by the way, the wearing of black would be far more appropriate than white. It's a shame you and your playmates here couldn't have been a little more appropriate." He made a tsking sound. "Did none of you people listen during your sensitivity seminars?"

He turned and went back to Lez. She stood at his approch, handed him his shopping bag, and as JB took her arm she said to the group, "Homophobic assholes.", then flipped them the bird. They left through the front door.

"I can't believe what a jerkwad he was..."

JB and Lez were back at Cherries, sitting opposite each other in the storeroom at her desk.

"What I can't believe is how the cops screwed this up," Lez said.

JB wasn't listening. "I mean, at first, I thought he might be a nice guy, but not anymore. How blatantly discrimatory can a person be? Maybe I should file a complaint." He looked over at Lez. She was still shaking her head in disbelief. "What? What did the cops screw up?"

Lez held up the baggy of Tom's belongings. "He had only a few things and they still got it wrong. This isn't all Tom's stuff."

She spilled the contents of the bag onto the desk. There were Tom's paint soaked briefs, an inexpensive watch, a gold ring, a lightening bolt shapped earstud, and a tiny shell shaped appliance.

"All this stuff is his..." She seperated everything but one object from the other ones. "...

but this isn't." She picked up a tiny flesh colored plastic appliance. "Tom wasn't deaf, so why on

Earth would he have a hearing aid?"

"It wouldn't surprise me if they did get it wrong." JB leaned forward to look at the things on Lez's desk. "But Tom had so little it should have been hard to make a mistake...even for the cops. Maybe he had it because he was listening to a Walkman. Can I see that?"

Lez handed over the device.

JB looked at the object. It wasn't a Walkman earpiece—there wasn't a place for a cord. In fact it did look to JB like a hearing aid. One of the kind that was undetectable when worn. "Lez, do you mind if I keep this? I want to show it to somebody who might know what it is."

Lez hesitated a moment and then nodded. Then her upper body crumpled onto the desk. Great sobs caused her shoulders to rise and fall.

"No, Lez. I'm sorry, you keep it."

She spoke with a wounded animal like howl. "That's not it, JB. Take it. I don't care. I just don't know what to do. Without Tom. I just don't know. What am I going to do?"

"Lez, you're still in shock. You need some time."

She looked up at JB, her face clearly filled with anguish and pain. "I don't care anymore, JB. About any of this. With Tom gone there isn't any meaning to any of it. I don't get it. Why did he do such a thing? Why?"

It was a question that had no answer. JB looked around the room—hoping there was someone to help him lurking in the stacks of boxes. Someone who could try to answer the unanswerable. That's when a knock at the door interrupted them.

"Tell them to go away, JB."

JB, glad at the interruption, went to answer

it. He found Scott standing at the door. Scott looked at JB's face and saw the discomfort riding his features. He gave JB a questioning look. Then he looked past him to Lez slumped at the desk. Realizing what her state must be he went past JB and over to her. He bent and warapped an arm across her back.

"Lez," he said, "it's okay. Hold on to me. Let it all go. Then we can try to make some sense of it. Let it go."

Suddenly, Crystal Van Ish, slightly silly fairy, had transformed into Mother Care, Earth bosom and keeper of the pain. He held Lez and rocked her like a child. As he did he somehow soaked up her grief. His momentary solace allowed Lez to breath again and she quieted in his comforting arms.

JB, grateful that someone better equiped than he to handle Lez's run amok emotions had taken over, softly asked, "Scott, who is Lez's doctor? She needs something to help?"

Scott reached across the desk with one hand. "They both used the same one..." He grabbed her Roladex, flipped to a card, and handed it to JB. "He can leave a prescription at the drug store. I'll go get it." He returned to soothing Lez.

JB took up the phone and moved away from Lez's hearing. Once the doctor was on the line he explained the circumstances and the doctor assured him sedation would be forthcoming. JB was about to hang up when he added, "Oh, Doctor, I have a question. Did Tom ever need or request a hearing aid? Lez said he didn't, but I wanted to check with you...I see. Well, thanks."

JB returned the phone to its place. Lez, still within the comfort of Scott's arms, said in an infinitely more rational tone than before, "I'm sorry, guys. I didn't mean to lose it there. I'm okay. It's all just so incomprehensible. Tom shouldn't have done something like this. It doesn't make sense."

JB sat back in his chair. "It was his illness, Lez. He heard a voice in his head, and that voice had control over him. He had no choice but to do what it told him. He was ruled by that voice. By his hallucinations, By that controlling omnipotent voice."

Lez leaned her head on Scott's shoulder. JB went on.

"It must have been like walking in a dream he couldn't wake up from. As sad as that is."

"My poor Tom. He could have...Now what is that?"

There was a knocking at the office door. Lez sat up straight. Scott stood and left them to answer it. Lez went on. "What I was going to say, JB, is couldn't Tom have said something to me? I could have helped."

"Not if the voice told him not to. Schizophrenics believe all sorts of things. He might have thought he was protecting you by not saying anything. Or that you might harm him if you knew. We'll never know."

Scott returned and sat across from Lez on the edge of the desk. "That was the beer distributor. For our order. I told him to come back later. But he did bring up a question, Lez. What happens to the bar now?"

"It's closed...at least for today. Probably forever. Actually, I don't care about this place anymore. It doesn't matter."

Scott shrugged his shoulders. "I suppose that's understandable for you, especially now. But it is a shame. This place is pretty popular."

"Do you want it? I'll give it to you. Just to be rid of it."

"You're joking?"

"Scott, I'm not in the mood for jokes. I'm a high school gym teacher from Burly, Idaho. What the hell am I doing running a gay bar in New York City? I mean it, do you want the place or not?"

"Well, sure. But, Lez, I don't have that kind of money."

"Don't worry about it. We'll work something out. I just don't want to be involved with this place anymore. Not without Tom. This was his place. It was what he wanted. I was only here because of him."

JB said, "Lez, if you want my opinion, you're in no state to be making these kinds of decisions." He stood, which caused his chair to scrape the floor. The sound echoed in the cavernous storeroom space. "What you need is some rest. Why don't you let Scott take you home? After that you can decide what you want to do."

Scott also stood. "That's a good idea, JB. We can stop and pick up your prescription while I walk you. Come on, Lez."

"It won't change my mind, but I am tired. I'll take your advice and rest. Let's go. But here, Scott." She held out her keyring. "You keep the keys. You'll need them to get back up to your apartment, what with the stairs being gone." Lez for a moment seemed to again lose her control, but stopped herself with an effort. "You'll have to use the elevator now, won't you?"

"That's right. We're going to need a new set of stairs."

Lez scooped up Tom's belongings from the desk, returned them to the baggy, and stored them in her shoulder bag. She looked around, then she went over to the wall of pictures behind her desk. She took down the framed photo of Tom and Timmy, hesitated over it a moment, then put that into her bag too. "Okay, let's go."

JB picked up his shopping bag and prepared to follow behind them.

"What's in the bag, JB?" Scott asked.

"Something I have to return to the store where I got it. It's in this area so I brought it along to save a trip back to my place."

They all left Cherries.

Chapter 21

Len wiggled his feet between the crisp starchy sheets of the hospital bed in his private room at Beth Israel and congratulated himself on finding a way out of the Equity charges mess.

It wasn't like he was the only actor to ever use this particular ruse. How many bad backs and flu's had his esteemed colleagues come down with over the years? And this had cost him. Plenty. Way more than just the couple of tickets to his play he thought he might get away with.

In fact, his doctor, though quite willing to help Len with his problem, had turned Grinch green with greed as he asked for his forty pieces of silver. He had insisted on not a couple of tickets to Len's show, but four tickets for the hit new musical that had opened to rave reviews down the street. Besides the theatre tickets Len had to subsidize dinner and drinks for the doctor's wife and another couple. Still, it was cheap at that.

Luckily, the hit musical's director happened to be Dalton Hughes, who had not only directed Len's show before the musical but Len had dated him a couple of times.

Calling on that relationship had allowed Len

to cajole Dalton into giving up his house seats for the night the doctor wanted to go. Of course, Len had to pay Dalton for the seats. Everybody thinks that house seats are freebies. Wrong. The person who had them kept for him also had to pay for them when they were used. If he didn't use them they got sold the same as regular tickets. And directors don't get nosebleed seats either, but prime orchestra. Fifth row center even. They cost Len around ninety dollars each.

Once the tickets were procured and the doctor was assured of a night to remember, Len had been admitted to the hospital for a "rest", and the newspapers were given the story that "exhaustion" was the cause of his missed performance. And that little *suggestio falsi*, when shown to Equity, would get him out of any charges and relieve him of any forthcoming fines.

Also, thanks to his celebrity and abundant charm, the nurses on the floor were thrilled to have him as a patient. They had all been absolute dears with their fawning over him. It was a real pleasure to be treated like someone special every once in a while. What was it Mel Brooks had said? "It's good to be king."

Len pushed the button to call his nurse, thinking a nice glass of something cool—lemonade perhaps—would be perfect. What arrived at the door wasn't his favorite scrub-dressed male nurse, and not what he had in mind at all. Standing in the doorway looking concerned—at least an eyebrow was raised—was Cubby.

"I read about your being here in this afternoon's paper. So I came right over. Are you okay?"

"Oh, Cubby, I'm fine. But come in. I'm so glad you're here. We need to talk."

JB opened the door to the Spy Shop and entered. Assuming he would meet the same rodent like clerk as last time he went up to the counter. Another clerk, older, thinner, more polished—less weasel like, more buzzard like—greeted him.

"May I help you, sir?"

"Yes, I'm afraid that I have to return this item I purchased." JB put the shopping bag on the counter.

The clerk looked over the rims of his glasses at JB. He felt like he was being sized up as a potential buffet. The clerk then took a look at the contents of the bag. He seemed to find both items, JB and the bag, totally lacking in any nutritional value. He looked up. "This is one of our best monitors. Did it not perform as expected?"

And now for a bit of equivocation, JB was thinking. He said, "Oh, that isn't the problem at all. I'm sure it works fine. What happened is the place where it was to be used has closed and the unit is no longer needed." The truth—having been bent in the right direction—will set you free. And might get you your refund.

"I see." The clerk studied JB for a moment and then took the camera box out of the bag. JB had been careful to repack it the same way it had been purchased, even down to the plastic bag wrappings on the inside.

The clerk opened the box, poked around carefully looking for damage, and finally said, "Well, I see nothing wrong with the unit so there should be no problem as long as it's within five days of purchase." He looked up to face the dated

receipt being held out by JB. "Yes, that will be fine."

JB handed the paper over and the clerk started the process. That was easier than expected, JB sighed relieved. There was always a slight sense of guilt when returning an item actually used but not wanted. Especially in this case, when there was no real reason for doing so—nothing broken, but the cost was way out of line with JB's budget. Besides, why keep it now that Tom was dead and the job had disappeared.

It took several moments for the clerk to get the paperwork done and to have JB sign everywhere. The cost would be charged back to his credit card. The clerk finally said, "That will do it, sir. I hope we can of service to you again."

"Actually, I could use some help right now."

"Fine. Is there something I might show you?"

"No, but there is something I would like to show you." JB pulled out the hearing device found on Tom's body. "Is this really a hearing aid, or is it something else?"

The clerk slid his glasses down on his nose and leaned over to see the object in JB's hand. He picked it up gingerly and held it closer to his eye. Then he dropped the item back into JB's hand. "That, sir, is a receiver...top of the line, in fact."

"Receiver? What do you mean?"

"It isn't a hearing aid. At least not like you mean. It isn't an amplifier, as would be used by someone who is hearing impaired. It is actually a small shortwave radio receiver, used as a communication device between two parties. In fact, the transmitting device is only slightly larger than the receiver. Let me show you."

JB followed the clerk over to a showcase. The clerk pulled out a box from the display and began to explain the intricacies of the device he was showing. JB hardly listened. His brain was spinning off in five or six directions, all trying to assimilate and put into perspective this new information about Tom.

"So you can see how easy it would be to misidentify the device. It could easily be mistaken for a hearing aid," The clerk finished.

"What?" Oh, yes. Thank you. You have been a huge help." JB took the clerk's hand in his, pumped it quickly, offered another thank you, and left the store.

Cubby sat on the edge of the cushioned chair beside Len's bed and looked up expectantly. "So, what is it we need to talk about, Len?"

Len took a breath, looked down at his hands a moment, and then looked over at Cubby from under his eyelashes. If this were a silent movie Len would be Lillian Gish flirting with her leading man in *Way Down East*. But this wasn't a silent and Len had the opening dialogue for this scene. "Cubby, we've been seeing each other for the last several months, and..."

Cubby nodded, obviously still not sure what road Len was going down."

"...and, I want us to be honest with each other. So, Cubby, here it is..."

The word honest must have triggered something in Cubby's head. His expression changed to concerned. Or was it guarded?"

"Cubby, I'm having some real feelings for you...beyond vocal coach and student, I mean."

Cubby leaned back into the cushions of his

chair, as if trying to put some distance—no matter how small—between him and Len. Most people seeing Cubby's evident discomfort would have stopped talking. But not Len. He plunged on.

"I realized this the other night, Cubby. I do care for you...a great deal...and I think I need to know how you feel about me. Is this thing between us going anywhere? What do you see ahead for us? Is there any future here?"

Cubby had taken on the look of an antelope drinking at the local Velt watering hole. Drinking, but fully aware of the beast on the other side of the pond. The one who wanted to eat him alive. "L-Len," he stammered, "I don't know what to..."

"Am I interrupting something?" JB was standing in the doorway to Len's room.

Cubby was on his feet instantly. He rushed over to JB, grabbed his elbow, and pulled him into the room. "No. No. Not at all, JB. In fact, I was just leaving. Len, I'll call. Soon. Real soon. Take care. Bye." And he was out the door.

JB looked after Cubby's retreating figure. "Who set fire to his ass? I didn't think he could move like that."

Len, with a bit of disappointment in his voice, said, "That, my friend, was the seldom seen, but oft rumored Gayus Committ-a-phobe-a-cus Run-away-a-sorus."

JB did his W.C. Fields impression. "Ah, yes-ss, spoken of in hushed tones by natives around the nightly fire. Known to disappear at the sight of a His and Hers bath towel set."

JB looked over at his friend expecting a laugh. Len's mouth was indeed set in a smile, but his eyes gave the lie to it. He was on the verge of tears.

"Len, hey, you did what you knew was best. You needed to look out for yourself."

"I know. But think of what we missed. We

could have been a pretty good couple."

"I've always thought the greatest lure to living in New York is how your life can change in the time it takes to snap your fingers. One moment you're out of a job, have no friends, and a bird has shit on your shoulder. The next you've sold your novel, hit the lottery for a million, and got asked out by an Adonis sitting on a slice of white bread. So who knows? Maybe Cubby will get his act together, and you two can be a couple somewhere down the line.'

Len wiped at his eyes. "God, aren't you Mr. Perky? I don't remember you being such an optimist."

"I'm not. I prefer to think of myself as a Hopeist. I always hope things will get better. I'm realistic enough to know that sometimes they don't. Like..."

"Like?"

"Like with this Fairy Dust serial slasher roaming the Village thing."

"Uh, need I remind you that the killer died in a fall just yesterday."

"I'm not so sure."

"Oh, Lord, here we go again."

JB sat in the chair next to Len. "When the police gave Tom's effects to Lez this morning this was in with them." JB set the device on Len's lap. "Tom was wearing it when he died. I checked, and it isn't what you think it is. It's a shortwave radio receiver."

"Why would Tom wear a radio receiver?"

"My question exactly. Unless? What if the voice Tom said was telling him what to do wasn't just in his head?"

"You mean sombody else was directing Tom by using a shortwave reciever?"

"It could be. Everyone was so amazed that Tom could have done the things the killer did. He didn't have what it took to hurt like this killer does."

"Well, I agree with that. Tom seemed like a real dyed in the wool mensch. Certainly not the type to pull wings off of flies."

"So, who's to say there wasn't another party to this Village killing spree? Another person who used Tom as a tool to capture the victims. Once Tom delivered a body this person would do the actual killing. It could have happened that way, right?"

"You're going back to the Village to check on this, aren't you?"

JB nodded. "I kind of have to. There are too many loose ends to just put this in a police folder and forget about it."

Len swung back the sheet of his bed, got up and went to the closet.He started changing from his pajamas to his street clothes.

"Len, what are you doing. You have to stay here, at least for the night."

"Why? I'm all right, The papers have alreadt reported I'm here, and as long as the nurses keep their mouths shut I'm still on the property. Besides, do you think I'm going to let you do this by yourself?"

"Len, I'm just going to Cherries to ask Scott a few simple questions. It's really no big deal."

"Then I'll just come back here when we finish up. I hate to admit it, JB, but I do get a kick out of this Miss Marple routine you've got going."

"Will you stop saying that? I can't be Miss Marple. I'm much younger than her and I hate tweed.It's itchy."

"Well, how about you be one of the Hardy

Boys in a taffeta prom dress?"

"How about Sam Spade? Anyone a bit less gay stereotypical."

"No. You're definitely the taffta type. Sorry abot that."

Chapter 22

Looking up at the naked stairless sidewall of Cherries JB tried to figure a way to let Scott know they were outside. "I suppose we could get some stones and throw them at the door," he said to Len, who was standing next to him. "That might get his attention."

Len started rummaging in his backpack. "I have just the thing," he said. He pulled out a brick sized black rectangular device and held it up.

"What's that?"

"My latest toy. It's a mobile cell phone." He pulled on a stub on the top and an arial came up. "Brand new in the stores. And a pretty penny it costs too. You really have to do something about getting yourself into the twentieth century, JB. What's his number?"

Len made the call and minutes later Scott came to the office door, let JB and Len inside, and took them up to his aprtment in the wire caged elevator.

On the way up JB told Scott what he had discovered about the hearing device.

"I knew it," Scott said. "Tom just couldn't have done those things. You get an idea of who a person is when you sleep together, and Tom wasn't that kind, at least not with me."

"I hope you're right, Scott. But it does make me wonder who it was that was controlling Tom then? If he was listening to a voice that told him to do things then that voice is still out there. And still as vicious as you say Tom wasn't."

"Then there might be more killings?"

"There could be, but I doubt it. This voice, whoever it might be, seems to be a clever S.O.B. And cowardly too. He used someone else to do his dirty work...to abduct his victims. Unless he has another someone like Tom, someone he can control in the same way, he's pretty much out of business,"

"Except for that unfinished business, JB. There is a body that hasn't turned up yet," Len added.

"That's right. The boy that was taken from the porn store. He hasn't been found yet."

Scott stopped at the refrigerator to get drinks while JB and Len went on into the living room and sat on the couch.

"What's all this, Scott?" JB was asking about a set of official looking papers that were piled on the coffee table in front of Scott's couch.

Scott handed over the drinks and said, "This mess is what Lez was talking about earlier. About selling the bar. She sent these papers over from her lawyers. I've been going over them for an hour and can't make any sense out of them. Mortgages, codicils, and legal jargon. Oh, my?"

JB threw up his hands. "Yipes, sorry, kid-do. I'd be no help at any of that. I have my own lawyer to look over my contracts. I could get him to call you."

"That could help, but.."

Len picked up the contract and scanned it. "It looks like a fairly standard wrap-around mortgage." He looked up, and seeing he had their attention, went on. "Scott, you'll have to make a down-payment...a fairly sizeable one at that... then you'll take over the existing mortgage plus a monthly payment to Lez. At the end the deed is signed over and you own the property. Not such a bad deal." He read a bit more. "Uh oh, I guessed as much. There's an exception. If you default Lez can make a thirty-day demand. That means you'll have to come up with the entire amount remaining or forfit the property back to Lez and lose everything you've invested. That's not usual, but it is legal."

JB eyed Len suspiciousily. "Where in the name of Leona Helmsley did you pick this up?"

"When you get home late from the theater you end up watching infomercials on television. It's the only thing that's on that late at night. Enough real estate pitches and a person is bound to pick up something."

Len put the papers back on the table. JB picked them up and began to look them over for himself.

"So, Scott," Len went on, "All in all, it isn't such a bad deal. The bank could dispute that exception, but at the interest she's asking for they probably won't."

Scott smiled. "It would be terrific if it worked out. The Rhino company would finally have a place all it's own to perform in. But that down payment? How much are we talking about?"

"Somewhere between affordable and *'You've got to be kidding!'* And that doesn't even begin to address the bar's liquor license. In New York another name for that city bureau is 'shut up and pay the graft.' You'll have to come up with a hefty amount of money up front."

Scott sat on the couch and slid down to rest on his shoulders. "Well, it was a nice dream while it lasted. I knew it was too good to be true."

Len shook his head. "Don't give up so easily. First, check all your options. There are bank loans, personal loans, even selling apples on the corner. And if you do come up with the money you'll need to make sure everything is kosher with those papers..."

JB spoke up. "Well, I've found something wrong already. This mortgage doesn't describe the physical property right."

"What?" Len leaned over to look at the papers. "That shouldn't be wrong. I spent some time working as a temp in a mortgage company and they were absolute fanatics about getting that kind of thing right."

"Well, this is wrong." JB put his finger on the paragraph he was referring to. "It describes the property as a three-story building and basement. There's only two stories and a basement, right?"

"Actually, that description is correct," Scott said. "Lez told me that when the building was built, back in the early eighteen-hundreds, it was three stories. The part that is now the bar...that you have to take the stairs to get down to...was the original first floor."

"So how did it end up being the basemant?"

"Over the years, what with the city paving new streets, installing phone and electric lines, not to mention sewer lines and subways...the street has been raised past its original level. So eventually this buildings second floor became the first, or the street level, and the first became the basement. There's a whole bunch of buildings like this here in the Village. This area has buildings that go all the way back to Colonial times."

"Then that means that this building has a sub-basement under the bar?"

"It does. It isn't used though. Maybe it could have been used as dressing rooms or something."

"Dressing rooms?"

"My idea was to change the cabaret room into a regular theater, with off-Broadway seating. We could have run real plays. That's what the Rhino Company does best. A drag show is fun, but plays are the meat of the group."

"So you want to be another Charles Ludlum?"

"Why not?"

"No reason. I suppose it's every little drag-princess's dream. To grow up and have a play-house of their very own. So why shouldn't you? Will the rest of the group go along?"

"Actually, we're supposed to meet in a half-hour to talk it over. At Trashy's place. You should come along Len. We need to talk about your cabaret act anyway. You too, JB."

"Uh, I haven't eaten yet, and I'm starving. I think I'll go over to Tiffs and get something."

"Suit yourself. Len?"

"Sure. I'll come."

Scott went to his bedroom to get dressed, which left JB and Len to wait."

Len looked knowingly at JB for a moment. Then he went over to the table where Scott's keys were lying. He picked them up, flipped through them until he found the one he wanted, took that one off it's hook, and set the ring back down.

"Here." He handed the purloined key to JB. "You'll need this when we leave."

"What for?"

"So you can get back into the building and check out that basement under the bar."

"Len?"

"JB? Come on, I know you too well. The minute that sub-basement was mentioned you were going to go down there. But, for crips sake, if you're going to play Jamie Lee Curtis at least take the key."

"Jamie Lee...what does the child of Tony Curtis and Janet Leigh have to do..."

"She's a horror movie maven, JB. There comes a time in every horror movie when the lady star goes into the old dark house. Even when she knows the killer or monster is waiting inside. Just be careful, okay."

"What are you worried about? I'll be out of there in no time. Hell, I'll be waiting for you on the deck by the time your meeting is over. But, how do we explain that Scott's key is missing?" JB remembered something. "Wait he has a habit of leaving his keys in the lock. That could cover it."

"Then I'll take care of it. Just leave it in the lock when you get in. I can schmooze him from there."

Scott came back then and the three of them rode the elevator down to the office floor, went out onto the deck, and said their goodbyes.

That left JB on his own. The sub-basement waited.

Chapter 23

Standing on the deck JB looked at the door into the building. It had, in just the last few moments, managed to take on an ominous and spooky feel. The door was a field of beaten and bruised metal with regular bumps of blackened bolts holding it to the frame. Swatches of rust running from red to orange were smeared across its battered front. Squint your eyes and that rust could almost be spelling out *"Go Back"* as if it was the entrance to the witches forest in the *Wizard of Oz.*

Shaking off the feeling as childish JB inserted the key and turned it. With a pitiful squeak the door opened onto the office. He put the key into his pocket and stepped in.

Desk shadows stretched across stained wood slats on the floor. Box nooks and storage crannies darkly filled the remainder of the space. Plenty of places for a killer to watch his every move. That shadow over there—it could be him. JB felt a shiver run through him. Get a grip, he told himself.

Behind the desk was the empty apace

where the picture of Tom and Timmy had hung just hours before. Before a distraught Lez shoved it into her bag and carried it away. It was a stark white square against the darker color of the rest of the wall.

JB went to the other side of that same wall and took the stairs down. At the bottom he stood looking out over the showroom. Lit only by the sconces that lined the walls the space had a cold and dank feeling. But it wasn't so much the decor as it was the temperature.

This wasn't the first time JB had noted the cold of this room, but it now took on a more sinister connotattion. The Fairy Dust Killer might have stored his victims in a room this cold. Kept them at this glacial degree to prevent their bodies from putrefying so quickly. The room really was as frigid as a morgue.

Now, where would there be an entrance to this alleged basement under the club? JB scratched his head. It would seem likely there was one in this room. But where could that be?"

Thinking back, he remembered the first time he had seen Tom. He had been hovering around this upper portion of the club's banquettes. Around this same area. It's just possible he had come up from this unseen basement.

Standard building construction practice said that if there are stairs going up to the upper floors there should be stairs going to a lower floor in the same locality. JB checked the area and found none. Suppose they were hidden somehow? Perhaps behind a wall panel that slid out of the way. Then there should be an opening device, right? It seemed a bit *Old Dark House* theatrical but JB checked the sconces for a trigger just the same. There was nothing.

Okay. So try putting yourself in Tom's place. He'd just left the porn shop with a body slung over his shoulder. He'd carried it stealthily and silently through the streets of the Village to here. Now he had to get it down below. Would he have still carried it? That would have been at least a hundred and fifty pounds of body to carry. And if the body was passed out it was dead weight. As strong as Tom was he would still get tired pretty fast. So what could he have done to make it easier? Would he have carried it down more stairs, or have used some other method? Something more expedient? An old coal chute maybe?

JB went back up the stairs. Then he went over to and out the office door. Outside, he made a close inspection at the back of the building. He checked to see if there might be an old coal chute square that had a metal cap that was easily removed, or bricks that were stacked without mortoe to hold them. He did find the chute but it was completely and sturdily bricked closed.

He went back to the door and turned the knob. Locked. JB looked for the key to turn but it wasn't there. Where was it? What did he do with it? He checked his pockets and quickly found it. This time he left it in the door as Len had told him to do.

Once back in the club he wandered about—thinking the problem out. There had to be an entrance to the basement. Where could it be?

On closer inspection JB noticed the ornately carved crown moldings that circled at the ceiling. Then he sighted other bits of Victorian style carvings—chair rails, dentils, plaster rosettes, and even a few cherubim. He realized the building actually still retained much of the original architecture.

So, go back to the original layout. To when this hadn't been a business but a residence. The floor where the bar and showroom now stood would have been a living room or parlor, there would also have been a library and a dining room.

So where was the kitchen? Behind the dining room? No, that's too modern. A hundred years ago it wouldn't have been considered proper for a middle class family with servants to have the kitchen on the same floor as the dining room. Too unsanitary. They would have used the basement as the kitchen.

And the servants would have had to carry all the food for meals up a flight of stairs? So they could drop the good china? I don't think so. Then was there a dumbwaiter in the original house? There must have been. Okay, a dumbwaiter. But where?

JB walked out into the center of the bar. Looking around he tried to imagine it as it was all those years ago. Where was the dining room? The parlor would have been at the front to take advantage of the street view. So the dining room probably would have been toward the back of the house. Back where the bar is now.

He walked to the bar and sat on one of the stools. A dumbwaiter?

The answer clanged into place. Of course. What's a dumbwaiter but a hand-operated elevator? And the bar does have an elevator. Used to transport items down from the storage room upstairs to this floor.

That elevator was probably put there because the shaft for it was already in the building. If the shaft was already there it should have run the entire length of the place, from top to bottom.

JB knew it went all the way to the top. But the bottom?

He got up and went behind the bar. On his knees he checked out the shaft. Looking up he could see the bottom platform of the elevator cage suspended on the floor above. Then he checked the wooden flooring at the bar level. This had to be the way down.

He squeezed his fingers between one of the slats and the concrete edge of the shaft. With only a minimal effort the slat loosened and lifted up. Minutes later JB had all the flooring slats removed, and was looking down into the dark of another floor. A floor below this one. That sub-basement did exist.

JB pushed the button to bring the cage down to the bar floor, and then went to search for the bar's flashlight. Most bar's had one. Not one of those simpy little plastic jobs you bought at the hardware store, but a heavy metal piece of equipment that not only can illuminate an entire room but also can knock the crap out of an unruly customer if needs be.

JB found the weapon and went back to the elevator. He stepped in, took a deep breath, and pushed the down button. The cage, with a groan, slid into the darkness below.

Nine feet later it came to a halt. JB clicked on the flashlight and found he was facing a set of wooden doors. Tall and heavy, they were pantry type doors that opened in the middle. At waist height there was an old fashioned latch. He reached out and pushed on the latch, then he stood back as the left door, now free, swung open from its own weight.

JB faced a large room. It was dimly lit by small blubs strung on loose wires along the ceiling joists. The unfinished walls were painted a slapdash black while white bits from the plastered laths showed through.

Able to see only the one wall from inside the elevator cage he spotted a stack of cans visble to him. The labels on them showed them to be a nationally advertised brand of paint filled with a bilious and unattractive shade of lilac that had become notorious of late. The killer must have stockpiled to prevent the police from tracing the paints actual purchase.

JB listened closely to hear if there was anyone else present in the basement. Any sounds of breathing or footsteps coming to see why the pantry door had swung open. What he heard was a slight rattle of chains. Chains?

He stepped forward to the front of the elevator and peeked carefully around the door.

The rest of the room was also painted black. It was furnished with the sort of equipment that was usually found in Christopher Street leather boutiques. There was a homemade rack screwed onto one wall, a leather harness was suspended from the ceiling over in the corner. A black vinyl and steel table with heavy straps hanging from its sides dominated the center of the room. Standing along side the rack was a twisted iron stand holding a large round black candle. An array of leather whips of various sizes and styles were displayed on pegs next to the stand. Chains of different weights were draped from hooks along the rest of the walls.

JB had heard of this sort of setup before. He had even seen one that wasn't quite so elaborate. This was a S&M afficionados perfectly appointed scene room. Called a Black Room, it was used for playing out sexual adventures exploring one's limits for pain.

What made this black room different was the dried lilac paint drips and splotches that spotted the walls and floor. This had to be The Fairy Dust Killers torture room.

Chains clinked again. JB realized the sound was coming from an alcove straight down along the same wall where he was standing in the elevator cage. He slipped out of the cage and stood hard against the wall. He waited to see if his movement had caused a like reaction from someone else. Not hearing anything he then slid along the wall toward where the clinking noise had come from.

At the edge of the alcove he stopped and listened again. He could hear a low barely audible moan. He quickly poked his head around the corner and then pulled back. There was a man hanging against the wall, chained up by his arms. He looked like a prisoner out of the Spanish Inquisition.

JB was sure it was chinoboy from the porn store. The boy in chino pants that Tom had carried away. Except the boy no longer wore his chinos. He was nude except for a ragged pair of jockey shorts clinging to his hips. His bare chest had been crisscrossed with slashes and welts from one of the whips displayed on the other wall. Blood had poured and dried from marks deep enough to have cut the skin. This wasn't S&M play. This was outright abusive atrocity. The boys head lolled to one side. His eyes fluttered as if he was on the very edge of consciousness.

JB not seeing anyone else in the alcove stepped out and went over to the boy. He set down the flashlight at his side and moved in closer.

Now what was his name again? Oh, yes, Keith. "Are you awake, Keith?" The boys eyes opened a bit and his head tried to come upright. "Good, I'll try to get you out of this."

JB reached up to begin working on one of the chains. That's when, from the side of his eye, like a ghost passing behind him, he saw a black gloved hand pick up the flashlight he had set down. Before JB could turn he felt a whack against the back of his neck. Then another hit. Then another.

JB felt all five of his senses go flying off into a blackness that quickly swamped his awareness. He started to lose the ability to stay standing upright so he grabbed onto chinoboy's shoulders.

The boy moaned pitifully as JB's hands slid down and across the cuts on his chest. The barely healed wounds were scrapped open and began to bleed once again. JB felt the boys Jockey shorts slide down with his hands as they went past his hips and on down the boy's thighs. JB's head stopped at the floor and rested on the boy's feet as he went completely out.

Chapter 24

Len stepped up on the deck of Cherries and took a quick look around. So where was the putz? JB said he would be here, and I don't see his skinny frame anywhere. Damn.

Scott, who was behind Len, moved past him to stop at the office door. He searched his keyring. "I have to have it," he mummered. "I know I had it when I left."

Len asked, "What is it?

"The key. I know I had it."

Len feigned exasperation and stepped in front of him. "Here it is. In the door."

"What? But how?"

"If you're going to be a bar owner you're going to have to be more careful with those."

Len stood aside as Scott bent to look at the lock. "Yeah. I guess you're right. Well, the ring must have broken. Oh well, at least we found it." Scott opened the door.

Len stayed outside. He was still hoping that JB would come around the corner. Maybe doing a buck and wing to prove wrong what Len was becoming more afraid of every second. Please, JB, prove me wrong.

"Are you going to come in?" Scott interrupted Len's dire imaginings. "Listen, I want to thank you again for what you're doing. It's a huge help."

Len went inside. "Oh, that? It's no big deal. The reason I'm doing the cabaret show isn't for the money anyway. It's supposed to get agents to start thinking of me as a musical performer. So, if any profit from the show can go toward you guys getting your theater, so much the better. Of course, a brass plate by the door extolling my generosity wouldn't be out of place."

Scott gave Len his expected smile. "I wouldn't count on that, dearie. But with your contribution and the last of my savings we'll be almost at a quarter of half of what we need. I see a huge yard sale in my future."

"Not a bad idea. Gay yard sales are the best. Sell all your old drag and accessories and make money. You could throw in any old antiques you have too."

"Old drag I have. No antiques though, unless we consider VondaLee."

"Hey, here's an idea. Maybe there's a bunch of old stuff in that sub-basement under the bar." Len could only hope he wasn't being too obvious.

"Could be. I was only down there once, and I didn't stay very long. Way too many creepy-crawlies for my delicate sensibilities."

"Is there a way down there from here? I haven't seen any stairs."

"There's a trapdoor behind the bar in the showroom. The stairs are under that."

That's it. That's what I wanted, Len mentally clapped his hands. He went on. "Well, you should check it out, Scott. It's a way to make some cash. Or, better yet, how about a rent party here at the bar? Charge people to get in a couple of nights. Once they know what it's for I'll bet they'll be glad to pay."

"Now that is a good idea. I'll have too..."

There was a knock on the outer door. Scott and Len looked at each other. Len shrugged, but was hopeful. Maybe it's JB?

Scott went to answer the knock.

"What can I do for you, Officer?"

Len, disappointed it wasn't his friend, couldn't hear the officers reply.

Scott said, "Oh, well, come on in. We'll try to help."

Scott came back into the office area followed by Detective Peters.

Len, was thinking, Humm, JB was right about him. He is gorgeous. But also, according to JB, a bit of a jerk too.

"Oh, It isn't there, Detective." Scott pointed at the empty white space on the wall. "Wait, I remember. Lez put it in her bag when we left. She was a mess after being at the police station. I walked her home."

Len said, "What is it? What do you need?"

The detective answered him. "I was hoping to check a photo we received this afternoon against that picture of Tom and his singing partner." He turned back to Scott. "Would it be possible for you to call Lez and have her bring it back here?"

"Sure." Scott went over to the phone.

The detective, looking a bit sheepish, said to Len. "I was hoping that JB might be here too."

Len thought to himself, you too? The detective finished, "There's something I need to explain to him."

Len said, "He was supposed to be here, but he hasn't shown up yet. Stick around, maybe he will."

"Okay. While I'm waiting though, there's this." He held out a photo. "It's a picture of the man Scott found in his closet. The mummy. The Swedish police sent this to us for identification."

Len took it and looked it over. The detective went on. "JB seemed to think there was some tie-in with the mummy and Tom. I brought that to prove him right...or wrong as the case may be."

"In that case, Detective," Len handed back the picture. "That guy. You're saying he was Tom's first victim, right?"

Scott, who was still on his call, added, "That's only a presumed victim, you know. There is no proof that Tom did anything."

Peters agreed. "He's right. But that's what JB suspected."

"Well," Len said. "The guy in that picture was a double for Tom's lover. Timmy. He had the same blond hair, the same build, even the same facial features. They could have been twins. So, Scott, I'm sorry, but it looks likely that Tom had some connection to the mummy."

Scott raised his eyebrows. "You'll have to have more than a picture to convince me Tom did all the things you people are accusing him of." Scott looked into the phone, turned his back on Peters and Len, and began to talk to the person who had answered.

Peters said to Len. "I think that JB was probably right when he said that this man was the first Fairy Dust victim. I think Tom picked him up, and for some reason, the whole thing got out of hand."

"So, you think Tom might have killed that man during sex that got rough?"

"Yes. I do. When Tom realized what he'd done he panicked and didn't know what to do with the body. So he wrapped him up and turned into a modern day King Tut."

Scott put down the phone. "I think that might explain the first victim, and I emphasize might, but it doesn't explain a bunch of other stuff about The Fairy Dust Killer case."

"Like what?" The detective seemed interested, not just indulging Scott's denials.

"Like why all the other victims were so different from this guy." Scott stabbed a finger at the picture in the detective's hand. "All of them have been a completely different type." He went behind the desk and sat. "Oh, and Lez said she'd be right down."

Len picked up on Scott's argument. "You know, Scott does have a point, Detective. Men seldom change their stripes or their types. For you straights a boob man is a boob man forever. For we gays its the same. For another thing, why were the other victims just tossed around the Village. Shouldn't there have been more mummies?"

Scott added, "Or, why was Tom wearing a hearing aid when he didn't need one?"

"Tom was wearing a what?"

Scott threw up his hands. "A hearing aid. He wasn't deaf, but when he died he had a hearing device in his ear. Didn't you know that?"

"No, but I haven't read the autopsy report yet."

Scott said derisively, "A little slow on the

up-take there, aren't you, Detective? Try to keep up with us. JB found out that the device was a radio receiver. So that meant Tom was probably getting directions from some other person. The real Fairy Dust Killer. Whoever it might be."

"Listen," the detective said, as he leaned on the desk "I don't think I like your attitude." Peters was facing Scott, who was sitting, so that he towered over him. Looking down at him, he added, "Beleive it or not, I'm trying to help you guys, and arguing with me isn't going to help. So cut it out. Now." He stood and softened his stance. "I understand that you cared about Tom, and you don't want to admit that he was this Fairy Dust person. But beleive me, if there was someone else involved, and that can be proved, we'll get them."

Scott not backing down, snorted, "And when is that going to be?"

Trying to play peacemaker Len interrupted the two men. "Hey, guys, Let's just calm down. You both have huge dicks and there is no reason to whip them out and prove it. I was thinking, what's back there in Tom's room? There could be a picture of Timmy. Why don't we check it out? You have the key, right, Scott?"

"It's here in the desk." He opened the center drawer. "His door is back there." He stood and passing the policeman led the way.

Detective Peters, following behind Scott looked back at Len. He seemed to be asking, What's up with him? Len shook his head and took up the rear.

Tom's room wasn't much. It was merely one long and one short plywood wall against the rear corner of the room. Scott opened the padlock, slipped the hasp, and pushed open the door. Peter's stepped up beside him and leaned in the door.

The contents inside weren't much either. It had a rumpled cot, a nightstand and a small lamp, and across the short end a rod for hanging clothes. The most disconcerting item was hanging from a nail on the wall above the cot. It was a V-neck sweater knitted in the infamous and now incriminating Fairy Dust lilac color.

The detective stepped into the room past Scott, who was still in the doorway. Scott said to him, "This doesn't look very good does it?"

Peters who now was staring at the wall opposite the cot, responded, "I'm afraid that this doesn't look any better."

Scott stepped into the room and turned to face the outer wall. An expression of shock came over his face as he sat heavily on the cot. "Oh, Tom, no."

Confronting them was an entire wall covered with a mad collage of ripped and torn papers. Newspaper articles, magazine layouts, tabloid coverage, and even flyers from lamp posts around the Village. Each had been pasted to the wall, one over another, in a sort of demented melange. Each of the articles detailed the murders done by The Fairy Dust Killer. Tom had then used a yellow highlighter to paint through pertinent passages. Even worse were the pictures of the victims. Tom had mutilated the pictures with a red marker—crossing out eyes, slashing mouths, obliterating noses. And in the center of it all, printed large in lilac paint were the words: *Please Stop The Voice!*

The detective said, "So you'll have to admit that Tom was, if not the primary person involved, then certainly an accessory."

Scott, still shocked at the brutality the wall

represented, nodded. "I don't have much choice now. But I knew Tom so well. And there is only one way I can think he was involved in this. He was manipulated by someone else. I still don't think it was Tom alone, despite what this shows." He waved a hand at the wall. "For him to instigated these kinds of savage murders isn't possible. Whoever did this is filled with more anger and hate than either you or I can even imagine. And that wasn't Tom."

"What he's saying, Detective, is that Tom was a gentle and kind man, and not capable of the kind of brutality exhibited by this killer." The two men looked over at the speaker. It was Lez, standing in the still open door of the tiny room.

Scott spoke to her quickly. "Lez, you don't want to see this." He got up from the cot and moved toward her.

"I already have, and it doesn't change the way I feel about my brother one iota. I still love him with every fiber of my being, and I don't know how I'm going to go on. That wall means nothing. It came from a person who wasn't himself. He was good, and..." Her voice cracked. She cleared her throat. "If anything, it was his illness."

She turned and went back to the front office area. She dug in her tote bag, pulled out a cigarette, lit it, and sat in her chair.

Scott followed Lez to the desk. Detective Peters closed Tom's door, then followed Scott. They stood side by side in front of Lez. Scott said, "Hon, you haven't heard all that JB and Len have found out about this whole mess. It will help..."

Peters laid Tom's key on the desk. "Speaking of Len, where is he? He was here with us just a few moments ago.

Chapter 25

Len found the trapdoor right where Scott said it was—behind the bar in the showroom. Lifting the trap gave him a view of precisily what he expected—your basic hole cut in the floor. Two stair treads made of not very sturdy looking wood planks were visible at the top of the opening. After that there was a great big dark. Even Jamie Lee Curtis would have hesitated over this hole.

Hoping that the treads didn't just stop after two, or have big gapping holes for him to trip into, Len took his first steps down. Relief momentarily replaced his analysis-sized anxieties as each step took him further into the darkness. Which then brought back the anxiety.

At the bottom his neuroses practically overwhelmed him. He was standing in a shoulder squeezing corner, as dark as the black thoughts that began to overtake him. Len's hands went out to touch the few inches available and he found only wall. Wall there. And there. Then he came upon an open space. He could breath again. More groping found it to be a hallway. He stepped into the space, totally blind as to what was ahead.

Odd, he was thinking, he'd expected it to smell down here—like something old or musty, like something hidden away for ages. But that wasn't the smell he was getting. It was a metallic coppery odor that hung like drying wash in the air. For some reason a faded memory floated to the surface of his mind.

By now his eyes had adjusted to the dark and he spied—in front and over to the left—a thin line of dim yellow maybe twenty feet straight ahead. He started moving again, aiming for that sliver of light.

Under his steps he could hear a crunching sound. It was, he fervently wished, dead leaves or something just as benign. But, more unsettling to his overwrought imagination, it could have been something alive, something that could bite at his exposed ankles, or worse yet, climb up a pant leg. Whatever the sound may have been didn't make his walk any easier on that over active fear of his. A fear that could easily conjure up an open pit of human eating crocs just waiting to eat his face.

The sliver of light turned out to be the edge of a door that hadn't been closed completely. Len pried it open and, lo and behold, he found another hall. He was beginning to think that he was Alice in *Down The Rabbit Hole*.

The doorways to several rooms lined each side of this hall. Probably maids quarters when the house was new, he decided. The dim light Len had followed like a Christmas wiseman was coming from a larger room down at the other end of this hall. He started walking toward it.

At the door of each of the rooms he could see

only darkness piled on more darkness. Some of the doors hung off their hinges, cobwebs abounded, and the occasional sound of little feet scurrying away brought back that creeped out feeling he'd been having.

Arriving at the end Len took a look at this better lit part of the basement. He took in the black walls, the home-made rack, the wall of whips, the torture table at the center. The worst of it was the smell. That coppery odor was stronger here. Len was finally able to put together where he knew it from. As a kid he had been prone to nosebleeds that would go on for hours. That was the smell. It was blood. Lots of it. The realization brought no comfort. "Well, isn't this festive?" he whispered to himself.

Then Len heard the sound of chains being rattled. Great, there were even sound effects in this chamber of horrors. His eyes followed the sound. What he saw was a tableau right out of the Marquise de Sade's little black playbook.

A young man hung from chains tied to a hook high up on the wall. He was nude, passed out, and bloody with whip marks across his body. Next to the boy, sitting on the floor and trussed up around his wrists and legs with more chain, was JB. A gag over his mouth prevented him from speaking, but his eyes were large circles of suprise at the sight of Len.

Len went over and bent down in front of JB. He put his hands on his knees and said, "I always knew there was a bit of the kink in you, old boy."

JB replied, "Mummmuphg."

"What's that? You're not being clear."

JB's eyes first narrowed then got wide. "Biesssuooo," he mumbled.

"What?", Len said holding a hand to his ear.

JB became agitated and began struggling against his chains. "Biesssuooo," he said again.

Len chuckled. "All right, JB. I'll take it off." He reached forward and pulled on the gag. The second it cleared JB's mouth he shouted, "Behind you, Len."

"What?" Len started to stand when a blunt heavy object crashed against the back of his shoulder. "Oowwww...damn, that hurt." He pivoted toward his attacker. "Now, what's this all about?"

"What I was trying to warn you about, Len."

"Well, why didn't you say so? Puny little thing isn't it. Hobbit sized."

Len's attacker, being several feet shorter than his target, had been aiming for the back of Len's head. He had missed when Len stood, saving him from a major concussion.

Now the attacker had to reach six-foot-twoish to connect with one of Len's soft spots. "I'm big enough to beat your ass," the attacker said, except the voice was mechanical sounding, as if Darth Vader from *Star Wars* was doing the talking. What Len actually heard was "Em beeg nuf do bett ya assss." The voice was high and sounded like a escapee from Munchkinland.

JB said , "Well, I wasn't ready for that. What the hell is with that voice. Is he on helium?"

Len laughed. "Don't make me lose concentration here, JB. This little guy has mayhem in mind."

Seeming to lose patience with them, or offended that they weren't taking him seriously, the attacker shouted, "I can still hurt you bad." Actuall: "Aie an ill tart you ad."

JB sat forward on his chains. "Obviously there's some sort of device to disquise his true voice. But it's coming across so high pitched. Why is that?"

Deciding not to use the basketball dunk approch on Len, the attacker held the flashlight he had picked up tighter in his hands. He shifted and swung it like a baseball bat. It came toward Len in a hard wide arc that aimed directly for his midsection. The attacker managed to connect squarely with his target.

Len, shocked by this unwanted invasion on his body, bent and grabbed at his stomach. "Oohoff." The attacker had knocked the air out of him. He struggled to take in air while feeling vulnerable and at risk to further blows. He slid to the side and as a reward for his fast thinking he received a deflected blow from the flashlight.

Now that Len was able to stand a few feet away from the guy he had a chance to see what exactly it was that was after him. He smirked. "JB is this guy loose from a road company of *The Leatherman's Follies* or what?"

His attacker stood about five feet four and was slight of build. But his attitude read as pure aggression. Sort of like if Bambi was a Mafia hitman. There was major aggression with nothing to back it up. He was dressed from head to toe in standard Anvil Bar black leather, including a full face zippered hood made of pieces stitched together like a crazy quilt. It gave his face a mad expression, very sinister at least from the neck up. The rest of his outfit—chained leather jacket, studded leather pants and motorcycle boots were ill fitting. Way too large they hung on his body and served only to camouflage his true form.

Further fashion critiques from Len were

superfluous when this maniac came running straight at him brandishing the flashlight like a wirrly-gig in a high wind.

Len braced his feet and let the attacker come at him. When he was within inches Len dropped his body and ran sideways straight for him. He hit the attackers body at chest height. Len lifted his body, using it as leverage, and flipped the attacker over his back. The attacker flew a few feet and landed solidily on his ass. He slid a few inches and came to a stop, causing the chains on his jacket to tinkle.

JB, mostly quiet until now, except for a few "Yeahs" to cheer Len on, said, "I've got it. I figured it out, Len. The attacker isn't a guy. It's a woman."

"And how, Sherlock, do you figure that?"

"It's the butt. A man's ass and a woman's ass aren't shaped the same. Being an ass man I shoud have seen that sooner. That is, believe me, a woman's rear end."

"You know, you could be right. I did feel something soft and bumpy in the chestal region when I flipped the bastard."

The attacker, now standing, was circling Len. Sidestepping him, making sure to keep some distance between them. She was aiming for the wall of whips.

She moved backward until she hit the wall, then reached out and grabbed hold of one of the lengths of braided leather. A flip of the attackers arm uncoiled a twelve-foot length of snapping dangerous lash. The attacker then reared back and heaved the whip toward Len. The snap of the end came within an inch of his right ear.

The attacker again reared back preparing to throw the whip a second time. But Len wasn't still where he'd been standing. He had used the attacker's preparatory pause to move against the same wall and grab one of the whips for himself. "Okay, bucko, so you want to play Lash LaRue do you? I'll play along."

Len let out a fierce yell as he reared back and threw his whip. But Len did it differently than the attacker had. His throw was quick, fast, repetitive. Each successive snap of the whip end got closer and closer to the attacker.

JB had a bemused expression as he asked, "Where in hell did you learn to use a whip like that?"

Len, slightly out of breath from his efforts, said, "I once played the Count of Monte Cristo in a play...but the finer points I learned from a couple of S&M buddies." Len again reared back.

A whip slash appeared on the attackers jacket, exposing the coat's red satin lining. More slashes appeared as the whip in Len's hand snapped at her again and again.

Snap. A slash to attackers calf. Snap, the knee. Snap, the thigh. Snap, the chest. Snap, the neck. Snap, snap, snap—driving, relentless. The barrage from Len's whip cracked in the silence like gunshots going off at a firing range.

This onslaught caused the attacker to sink down into a crouch, bringing up her arms to protect her head. Finally she laid down and pulled into a ball as the only way to find some relief from Len's whip.

That's when they all heard the turning of the gears and wheels that carried the elevator first up and then back down the shaft.

Chapter 26

Lez grabbed the brandy decanter from its display place behind the bar and poured herself two fingers. The drink was in reaction to what Scott had just told her. That Tom had been manipulated to do the kidnapping's by someone else.

She had listened calmly as Scott explained. She contemplated its meaning. Then she stood and walked to the stairs. That left Scott and Detective Peters to follow her. She headed straight for the bar. Not the showroom bar where she would have had to take the time to unlock the booze, but to the main bar where her personal brandy bottle was kept.

She figured she deserved a drink. Having one would also give her time. The time it took to get a glass, to open the bottle and to pour it was the right amount. It gave her a moment to examine this new information. What Tom's involvement in the Fairy Dust Killing's actually was.

And who wouldn't need a drink when you had just been told your beloved brother, now dead, had been so cruelly used? That it hadn't been Tom who was responsible for the awful things he was accused of. That Tom was under the control of some other son of a bastard, asshole, mother-fucker who had made Tom jump to their pervert-ed commands. That Tom had been simply a worm on a line.

Lez poured herself a second shot of brandy. She slid the bottle over to Scott, who poured a splash of liquor into his glass.

"Are you okay, Lez?" He sipped at his drink.

"I'm in shock, Scott. I don't get it. If Tom didn't do this then how do we get the cowardly murdering scum that did do it?"

Peters stepped up to the bar. "Lez, as I told Scott, you need to understand that what JB has come up with here is purely supposition. A theory at best. There is no proof that there was anyone else involved in these killings."

"What about the hearing aid? That's proof."

"That he wore a hearing device. That's all. And the fact he did doesn't really relate to the killings."

"Officer," Lez pleaded. "I'm grasping at straw here. And now you're telling me I can't spin it into gold?"

Scott abruptly turned away from the two. His head went to the side as he listened.

"What is it, Scott?"

"Nothing, I guess. I thought I heard gun-fire. There have been fire bombings and pot shots taken at other bars here in the Village. Homopho-bia in action. I get paranoid. It was nothing."

That's when all three of them heard a rapid series of popping sounds.

"Well, that isn't nothing," Detective Peters said. He checked to make sure his firearm was where it should be "But it wasn't gunfire. It isn't loud enough."

Lez asked, "Where's it coming from?"

Scott said, "It's from under us. Could it be the subway?"

Peters said, "Hell, it could be someone making popcorn. But why in the basement?"

Detective Peters turned to Scott, "You know, I'm still wondering where Len is?"

Scott looked at him. "Maybe you're right. Before Lez got here he was asking about that sub-basement."

Lez pointed to the elevator behind the bar. "Look. The floorings been pulled up. That's odd. And the cage is down there."

"You don't suppose Len went down there?"

Peters responded, "Considering what my captain has told me about both Len and JB it wouldn't surprise me in the least."

They heard another series of quick pops.

"Damn it, what is that?"

Scott looked at the detective. "There's one way to find out." Peters nodded.

Lez went over to the elevator and pushed the button to bring the cage up. It started to rise. When it stopped Scott and Peters stepped on. Scott reached forward and pressed the down button. He looked at the policeman. "Maybe you should get out your gun, Detective. We might need it."

Lez watched as their heads disappeared down to the sub-basement.

Neither Scott nor Peters had any idea what

they were going to find when they hit the bottom of the elevator shaft. It could be nothing. It could be a gang of thugs. Or it could be Len pulling some twisted joke. Whatever it might be they prepared for the worst.

Detective Peters drew his weapon and stationed himself toward the front of the elevator. He bent slightly at the knees and held his gun chest high with both hands, so that his position also served to sheild Scott from any danger.

As the cage came to a stop the detective used his right foot as a battering ram to kick hard against the double doors that enclosed the elevator. Both doors swung open, hit against the outside walls, and swung back closed.

"Now that was clever. Are we trying to confuse the enemy?" Scott snorted. "Maybe we shoud gently push this time?"

Peters, irritated, said, "Yeah, well, whatever works." He again prepared for what might be outside the doors. Taking his position he jerked his head at Scott. "You do it this time."

Scott stepped to the doors, stood so he was sidways to them and pushed ever so gently.

Peters lept out into the room and stopped in a crouch. He swung his body first to the left, then over to the right, surveying the room. He stopped at the right, looked straight ahead for a moment, then he stood.

Scott, seeing the detective relax his guard, took a cautious step out of the elevator into the basement. After his own survey he gazed in wonder at what was laid out before him.

The two men were confronted with a scene lifted from the last chapter of a Nineteen-thirties Saturday afternoon serial. Captain Jack Studley and the Black Bandit.

Len was standing in the center of the room facing them, His turned in heroic profile, his feet spread, with a bullwhip held in one hand. Missing only the Indiana Jones fedora he was the hero of the serial.

In front of Len there was another person, presumably the villain since the apparel from head to toe was all black. This villian was crouched down with their arms over their head as protection from the fury of Len's whip. His lash had already left cuts and slashes across the back of the villian's jacket.

A few feet behind Len, taking the damsel in distress part, was JB. He was on the floor hogtied with a length of chain held tight with a sturdy lock. Next to him was another boy. He was nude, passed out, and hanging from the wall by another length of chain.

Len took his eyes from his hostage for a quick moment. "You two could use some practice on your entrance, but I'm real glad you're here. His attention was drawn by a movement below him. He took a step back and snapped the whip over the villian's head. "Don't even think about it, sweetheart," he said. The hostage squatted again.

Peters, mystified by it all, asked, "Who's going to explain what the hell this is about?"

JB from the floor, answered, "It's pretty simple. I came down here to check it out, and that idiot over there attacked me and tied me up. A little later Len showed up."

"To try to find JB."

"And he was attacked the same way. But he was able to fight back. He, shall we say, whipped the assailant into a corner. Magnificently, I might add."

Len took a bow while still watching his hostage.

"And, we've been like this until you guys arrived."

The detective asked, "But who is that?"

"Oh, sorry,"JB said, "I thought that was clear. That's the real Fairy Dust Killer. The one who controlled Tom. She actually did the murders."

Peters said, "She?"

Len looked at the detective. "As enlightening as this all is, could you do something about incapacitating this bitch? My arm is tired and doesn't have a hell of a lot of snap left in it."

Peters reached into the back of his coat and pulled out a pair of handcuffs. He went to the killer, grabbed hold of the shoulders, lifted, and slipped the cuffs on her wrists. The rasping of the metal cuffs as they closed echoed in the room.

"Uh, while you're at it, Detective," JB said, "That chain looped at her waist leads to a set of keys. One of which will open the lock on these chains. Could you maybe find it and release me?"

Peters pulled on the chain, ripped it from her pants, and went over to JB. He bent and tried one of the keys. Not that one. Maybe this one? "Uh, JB, could we have a talk after this is over? I need to explain something."

"What? Not now."

"That's what I mean. Later. Can we talk?"

"All right, Sure. But right now please get me loose." Peters went back to trying keys.

Scott had taken over guarding their hostage from Len. He took hold of the zipper at the back of the hood and started to open it. "Enough already," he declared. "I want to know who this person is."

JB looked over at him. "Well, I already know that. What I want to know..."

Scott lifted the leather hood from their hostage's face. It was DeDe.

"...is what her ex-husband looked like?"

Len, now finished with his whip duties, was removing the boy from the wall. The boy uttered a moan when his arms were released. Len sighed with relief, thankful the boy was alive. Spotting a blanket over in the corner he covered the boy. Then he looked at JB. "He's going to be okay, I think. But why do you want to know about her ex?"

JB was unwinding the chain from his legs. "The husband is what this entire thing had been about from the beginning Her ex was a habitual abuser and batterer. I'll give you odds he was dark haired and swarthy too.That's why Tom was picking victims that went against his type. It was her revenge, not his, that was being played out."

The chain now off JB stood and went to DeDe. "That's what it was, wasn't it, DeDe? Hate and fear and abuse...both physical and verbal I'll bet. This was revenge against the man who hurt you so badly. It was his death, his cries for mercy, his torment every time you killed. Then you followed it with the mutuilation. The tongues. So they would remain silent? Oh, DeDe, what monumental hurt you must carry around inside you."

DeDe, so far, had been making little more than guttural sounds. Hums and mews punctuated by grunts. JB standing in front of her, gave cause for her to stand up to her full five-feet-four inches, snort, and spit at him.

JB wiped at his face. "Okay, DeDe, You'll get no sympathy from me then. You do know it's illogical to kill those you hate, because when they're dead they are beyond any pain you wanted them to feel. So what did you accomplish? Huh?"

"Uh, gentlemen, we need to get her to the station," Peters said. "Why don't Scott and Len go up first, then JB and I can bring up the woman after I read her rights to her."

Two rides up and down brought Scott and Len to stand protectivly by Lez, while JB, Peters and DeDe rode to the main floor. As the elevator stopped at the bar JB opened the cage door.

When DeDe saw Lez watching them she backed as far as she could into the shadow of the cage. JB said to her, "You're going to have to face Lez sometime. You may as well do it now." Peters took hold of her arm and moved her out to the front of the bar.

JB noticed that Scott, standing next to Lez, had his arm around her shoulder. He couldn't tell if it was from sympathy or was meant as restraint, because Lez looked like she might commit mayham any second. Her face was screwed into a mask of hatred, giving her the look of a pissed-off Kabuki warrior.

DeDe, bent at the waist so she wouldn't have to look Lez in the face, stood in the center of the bar. JB went to get a barstool for her to sit in. Peters said, "Get one with arms. I can cuff her to the slats." Picking up the requested type of stool JB sat it in front of DeDe. She hissed at him, sounding like a cat ready to strike.

"Sit," Peters ordered. He unlocked one of her cuffs and hooked it to a chair slat. Then he did her other arm with a second set of cuffs. She couldn't run anywhere with a barstool attached to her wrists. With DeDe well secured, Peters went to the bar and picked up the telephone.

Once his call was answered he said, "Sagge? Peters here. I'm going to need a squad car for a perp and an ambulance for a vic. At Cherries on Christopher. ASAP. We're in the downstairs bar. Yes. All right." He hung up and returned to stand next to DeDe with JB.

An awkward silence prevailed as they all stood uncomfortably in their places. None of them knew what to say to break the tension that was blanketing the room.

Then Lez broke off, went over to the bar, and poured herself another drink, while staring daggers at DeDe. DeDe sat with her chin down, refusing to look at anything but the floor. Peters and JB, standing behind DeDe, took peeks at each other while trying to figure out what to say next and who should say it first. Scott, now sitting next to Lez at the bar, looked to Len. Len looked back and shrugged.

The scream from the ambulance siren pulling up outside thankfully then grabbed everyone's attention. Scott took out his keys. "I'll unlock the door for them." He crossed the bar and climbed the stairs, where he waited on the landing as the paramedics came to the door. Seeing they had brought their mechanical gurney he had to tell them that it wouldn't work where the patient was. They went back out to get a wooden stretcher. Then Scott directed them down to the bar. He yelled to the people down there, "I'll stay here. The police should be here soon."

Len met the paramedics and led them to the elevator cage. He filled them in on what they would find down below as they stepped onto the platform. He then pushed the button and watched them disappear down the shaft.

Peters had taken several steps back from

DeDe and motioned to JB. He went back and stood beside the policeman. "All right, Detective, you wanted to say something. What is it?"

Looking uncomfortable, Peters said in a low voice, "First, JB, I want to apologize for that crude remark I made the other day."

JB nodded. He waited for the excuse that always came next.

"But you have to understand, I work with those men everyday. If I'm ever in trouble I have to depend on them to save me. If those guys should even guess that I'm really gay I can't do that anymore. It's happened before, to other cops."

JB had to admit that as far as excuses went that was a pretty good one. Peters finished, "But, I was hoping we could, uh, that we might, uh, go out?" Damn a shy Peters was even more desirable that the regular one, but JB had to say what he had to say.

"Detective, I'll be honest, I can't begin to understand what you have to endure on your job everyday. But I do know that it's been a long road for me to be out and to take pride in who I am as a gay man. And I won't go back. Now you haven't begun to walk that road, and I don't blame you for that. But I won't compromise where I am either. I don't want to hurt your position, so I can't see where we have much of a chance."

The wa-wa wail from a police car was heard pulling up outside. Scott, who was still standing on the landing, yelled down, "Lez! No!"

No one had noticed in all the hub-bub of the paramedics and the police arriving that Lez had left her place at the bar. No one noticed as she walked across the floor to where DeDe was sitting. No one noticed the small gun Lez held in her hand.

JB and Peters looked over at the two women. Lez stood in front of DeDe. One of her hands held DeDe's chin. The other hand held the gun to DeDe's forehead. They didn't have time to get to Lez before...

The gun made an unexpectedly soft sounding pop, like a selzer bottle being opened, when Lez pulled the trigger.

DeDe, at first sat straight, stiff with shock, then she slumped in her chair. Her head leaned to the left. There was a small opening going directly into her brain. A slight trickle of red poured from the tiny hole. However, the other side of DeDe's head had been blown wide open from the bullet's exit. Blood, brain tissue, and skin were spattered over several feet of the floor around her. The smell of hot seared flesh filled the air.

Scott ran down the stairs and over to Lez. He grabbed her shoulders and shook her. "Lez, my God, what were you thinking?"

Lez, calmly looked straight ahead past Scott and the rest of the room. In a colorless voice she said, "The bitch killed my brother."

Epilogue

The spotlight caught the shine from Len's hair, which caused a bright aurora to surround him. He sang the first few notes of a Jacques Brel song, in French yet, as the rest of the Rhino troup acted as back-up singers. Accompanied by piano, guitar, and drums the whole effect was professional edging close to spectaular.

The last few weeks, since the capture and death of The Fairy Dust Killer had, to say the least, been hectic for Len, Scott, JB, and the rest of the gang.

Lez, being charged with murder in the second degree in DeDe's death, had resulted in Scott being offered an even better deal than before for the purchase of Cherries bar. Her need for bail money had required a heavier up front amount, but way less on the back-end. Scott had hocked everything he and the rest of the Rhino company pocessed to get their part of it. He hadn't managed to come up with quite enough, but was then able to find two investors who agreed to become silent partners in the venture. JB and Len figured an investment in a Village theater could end up making a profit, besides the money was just sitting there making interest anyway. Helping to further the cause of gay theater wasn't such a bad reason for giving up their savings.

Lez did make her bail, and had used every spare penny to then get her lawyers to claim everything from diminished capacity to temporary insanity.

The past few weeks in and around the bar had been filled with workmen doing their thing to turn the showroom into a real theater. It had just managed to meet the deadline for it's re-christening as The Rhino for Len's opening.

Now it was up to the critics to decide if out of the chaos came an act, as the lights went up on The Aardvark Varieties.

JB sat in his seat watching the show with another person. Next to him was now ex-detective Needham Peters soon to be security consultant Peters. He had decided to leave the force so he could life a life of pride. It was a commodity JB had for him in abundance.

In fact, JB had been thinking what a good idea the entire situition would be for his series of mysteries. Something along the lines of Sue Grafton's alphabet stories. Except JB's hero is a man who lives in New York and is gay. Q for Queer, P for Pansy, S for Swish, Hummmm

About the author:

Ken Lansdowne has lived in California, Nevada, New York City, New Mexico, and now lives in Denver Colorado.

The first novel in *The Bent Mystery* series is *Secrets Don't Belong In Closets*, the beginning. Second is *A Murderous Ball of Fluff. The Fairy Dust Killer* is the third. Fourth is *Home Sweet HoMo.* Fifth is *Dance:Ten Murder:Maybe?.* Sixth is *A Mystery, Wrapped In A Mystery, Surrounded By A Mystery.* Seventh is *The Art Of Death,* and number eight is *Bathhouse Bloodbath!*

There is also a Gay themed Christmas novella: *Jacob Marley*

If you would like to get an automatic e-mail when the next book in the series is ready for release sign up at k.lansd@outlook.com. Simply put the word "LIST" in the subject line of your email. Your e-mail address will never be shared and you can unsubscribe at any time.

Word-of-mouth is crucial for any author to succeed. If you enjoyed the book please consider leaving an online review, even if it is only a line or two: it would make all the difference and would be very much appreciated. If you didn't like it I apologize for taking up your time: my purpose was only to entertain or give you a laugh or two.

www.ingramcontent.com/pod-product-compliance
Lightning Source LLC
Chambersburg PA
CBHW070820120626
46556CB00002B/597